ARROWHEAD

LIBRARY

SYSTEM

THE FIDDLER

THE FIDDLER

DAVID KING

DOUBLEDAY & COMPANY, INC.

GARDEN CITY, NEW YORK 1978

To set the record straight on a matter that may be of concern to history buffs, the characters who people this book and the related events are fictional, although it all might have happened within the framework of those fabulous years when Virginia City, Nevada, was this country's gold capital.

Library of Congress Cataloging in Publication Data

King, David, 1914–
The fiddler.

I. Title.
PZ4.K52146Fi [PS3561.I475]   813'.5'4
ISBN: 0-385-13438-x
Library of Congress Catalog Card Number 77-12861

For my son Peter

THE FIDDLER

I

The fiddle screamed like a gutted cougar. The caterwauling had been going on for an hour since the blazing sun went down. It came from the lockup's big pen which, on Saturday nights, accommodated the roundup of Virginia City's brawlers. This Wednesday night only four men were confined but they were raising seven kinds of hell.

"Bejesus, Cyrus!" the deputy hollered and rocked from the tilted chair to his heels. He was hot and edgy. "That's pure agony. I'm going to bust that fiddle over that polecat's head."

Panting and sweating, he started for the slab door that stood open to the corridor between the jail's three cells and the pen. His shirt was plastered to his back like a wet leaf, and the band of his flat-crowned, fawn-colored hat was a moist thong about his forehead.

"Calm yourself, Bart," Cyrus Fargo told him, and the deputy turned his head to the town marshal. Bart saw a thin smile touch Fargo's stern lips but his cold-steel eyes reflected no humor. Grizzled, he was tall and inflexible behind an oak desk. After twelve years of service, Bart knew well that the marshal was a man without mercy, yet Fargo said, "In a way, I've got to admire those four. If you knew you were to meet death in the morning, do you think you could ride out so brave, a-fiddling and a-singing? Besides, so long as we can hear them, we know they aren't brewing up some mischief."

"I'll close the door," said Deputy Bart Axelrod, and he put his hand to the slab. The gesture was tentative. He needed the marshal's approval for every move he made. "Maybe that will help."

"Nope." Marshal Fargo spoke quietly but his voice carried as much authority as the Army Colt .44 that lay at his hand. "They got sparse air. There's just that one small window in the pen. There's scarce a breath tonight. It's hotter'n the hinges of hell. We leave that door open for what draft there is."

"It ain't like you, showing favors to the prisoners," Bart complained, but he knew it was useless. He clomped back to the chair against the wall.

"Justice can be tempered with compassion," the marshal declared.

"Bosh!" Bart said. Consideration for criminals was an unaccustomed gesture for the marshal. Normally he was indifferent. "You always said a prisoner's got no rights and a condemned man is already dead. What's got into you tonight?"

"This is their last night," Fargo said.

"What the hell difference that make to you?" Bart demanded. "You always said a criminal should suffer the same hurt he brought to his victims. You said never show a weakness to a prisoner, and kindness is a weakness. The very words."

"There are exceptions," Fargo said without explaining.

"You make exceptions for them four thieves and murderers?" Bart was confused and angry. Accusingly, he said, "You shouldn't of left that window in the pen unshuttered."

"Closing off the window on such a night would have been inhuman."

Bart snorted. "Since when you been human? I seen you pistol-whip a prisoner for passing gas." He chewed his cheek, worrying about that window. "Their friends could pass a gun between the bars."

"Of what use is a gun to them?" the marshal asked coolly. "Only one of us goes out there at a time. If they showed a gun and demanded the keys and we refused, all they could do is kill whichever one is there. The other would take a rifle and shoot them all like fish in a barrel. Now use your head, Bart. Would a gun get them out?"

Bart hesitated. "Supposing that one of us didn't refuse?"

The marshal's eyes frosted. "I'd refuse," he said, hefting the .44. "*You* would. The window stays unshuttered, the door stays open."

Bart blew out his lips in protest. "What difference a little heat to them? They'll burn in hell tomorrow, once we dangle them from the courthouse balcony."

"Let them have what comfort's left," Fargo said with finality.

Bart was beset. Everything the marshal said and did was contrary to his nature. Fargo seemed well disposed to the outlaws: Two-finger Jake, Montana Mac, the Carson Kid, and the Fiddler. "Four of the West's most desperate badmen," the handbills read. Wanted, dead or alive, for an assortment of crimes that included bank, stage, and train robberies. Bart did not know the particulars. All he knew was, the band had raided the Miners' Bank at Virginia City and the marshal had apprehended them single-handedly. The three in the bank had offered no resistance, and the Fiddler, who was on the street and not suspected, had turned himself in as the leader of that crazy bunch. The out-of-town, out-of-state notices made no difference. Bank robbery was a hanging offense in the sovereign state of Nevada. The outlaws had been quickly found guilty by the miners' jury whose gold was in that bank. The four had spent only two days in the hoosegow, and tomorrow they would die.

While Bart and Fargo had been talking, the Fiddler had begun to saw away at another tune. Bart saw the marshal recognized "Crydersville Jail" because his faint smile came and went again. The men were tapping their boots and singing:

> *I said, Mr. Jailer, please lend me your knife,*
> *I said, Mr. Jailer, please lend me your knife,*
> *For the lice and the bedbugs have threatened my life.*

Fargo laughed aloud. "I take off my hat to men who can josh like that the night before they're hung. You wouldn't have denied them this last pleasure, now would you, Bart?"

"Sure I would," Bart said hotly, "and you would of, too, if the heat hadn't gotten to you and made you fuzzy in your thinking. You shouldn't of give them that fiddle."

Another fleeting smile quirked the marshal's lips. "Why? Because it discomforts you?"

Bart thumbed back his hat. "Hell, yes, it does. It makes me sick. But that ain't it. There might of been something inside."

Fargo's smile was tolerant. "I considered that," he said placidly. "There wasn't."

Bart's concern was real and he felt it in his marrow. "There's more than meets the eye to this," he said obstinately.

"You got a lot to learn," the marshal said. "Those men in there started out life good people, same as you and me, but something put them wrong. We don't know what faulted them but they weren't always bad. Somebody gave the Fiddler a violin once, and he took to it."

"He probably stole it," Bart muttered.

Fargo seemed to ignore the interruption to the philosophic mood that had captured him. "Maybe, if things had been different, the Fiddler would be in a concert hall tonight instead of playing his swan song here."

"It don't matter one damned bit," Bart sputtered. "He's due to hang, and the Preacher brings him a fiddle instead of a Bible. It ain't natural."

"Oh fiddlesticks," the marshal said and chuckled as if pleased with the joke he'd made.

Bart made a sour face and went silent. He couldn't argue with the marshal but he could show his disapproval. Cyrus had been doing the wrong things all evening. About an hour earlier, with the setting sun glowing like an ember in the banked furnace of the coming night, a squint-eyed runt in a black vest and wearing a black string tie had hobbled into the office. A tattered, rusty hat was in one hand and fiddle and bow were tucked under a withered arm. Bart did not like the looks of him but he wore no gunbelt. Bart didn't recognize the man but his type came and went like shadows in the night at Virginia City, the gold capital of the West and perhaps the world. This one, at least, had not been in local trouble.

"Would you grant a condemned man a last request?" the halfpint somberly asked the marshal.

Bart expected Fargo to snap a flat refusal, but instead he said reasonably, "If it's not outlandish."

The peewee transferred his hat to the clutched fingers of his shriveled arm and removed the fiddle and bow, which he extended to the marshal. "Fiddler Frank is kin," he said apologetically. "It has always been his wish that when his time came he go to a lively tune and dance upon the gallows. Would you allow him the solace of his fiddle on his last night?"

"If you've not hidden a gun or knife inside," Fargo said good-naturedly. He took the fiddle and shook it. "I'll see he has it straight away. Who will I say left it?"

The pipsqueak sloshed on his hat. "He'll know, but if it's you who's curious, I'm known as the Preacher." He started out but turned at the door. "Bless you, Marshal," he said solemnly before he left.

Fargo had seemed pleased with himself when he took the fiddle back to the pen but Bart distrusted the visitor. Now he said, "Do you think they are kin? The Preacher and the Fiddler? Maybe we should of throwed that little guy in with the rest of them. He could be in the bunch."

"Nonsense," the marshal said. He sounded annoyed.

"Maybe we ought to close and bar the front door," Bart suggested.

"What for?" Fargo asked crossly.

Bart scrunched his eyebrows together. Damnit, he didn't like nor understand Fargo's lackadaisical attitude. "The Fiddler and his gang might be planning something."

"Planning what?"

"Jailbreak," Bart snapped. "The door's wide open. The Preacher walked right in on us. A dozen armed men could do the same and break them out."

"Mule's milk!" Fargo barked. "Stop your carping. You're trying to nag me into taking away that fiddle. I won't do it. Lean away, Bart."

"All right, Cyrus," Bart growled, "but don't say I didn't warn you."

The Fiddler had scraped into another ballad, and the outlaws' lusty voices implored:

Slack your rope, hangman, slack her off for a while,
I see my daddy ridin', ridin' many a mile.

The marshal laughed heartily. He seemed to enjoy the dark humor of the condemned men. Bart pushed his hat over his eyes and tilted the chair back against the wall. Fargo appeared to like the Fiddler. The Fiddler puzzled Bart. He didn't look nor act like an outlaw. He was tall and lean, powerfully built of sinew and rawhide, but otherwise his appearance was gentle. Abundant waves of yellow hair cascaded to his shoulders and softened finely chiseled features. Deep-blue eyes were clear and met a man's straight on. His manner was forthright and he appeared to be a guileless young man who'd taken a wrong turn along life's devious pathway. That would be when he'd fallen in with the other three. They were the meanest lot of hard-cases Bart had encountered since he took his oath from the marshal back in the territorial days.

The marshal still was the only law there was north of Carson City, and Bart was proud of the part he'd played in shaping Virginia City. From the discovery of the Comstock Lode in '59, he'd fought vigorously with Fargo to prevent Virginia City from spawning another claptrap mining camp. He'd steadfastly sided the marshal, who'd enforced the law with unremitting zeal and a smoking Colt. Fargo had often said he meant to structure Virginia City into a model community of decency and permanence, a place where people would be proud to be born, prosper, and die in peace. Together, they'd laid a sound foundation.

Despite the squalid alleys of board and batten miners' shacks and the sordid saloons that peddled cheap whiskey

and fancy women, Virginia City was a respectable munici-
pality and Fargo and he kept it that way. The outlaws
would be hanged in the morning as a warning to the law-
less that their breed would not be tolerated. The courthouse, where the event would take place, was a two-story
building of substantial sandstone. The Miners' Bank also
was built of sandstone and stood two stories tall. Its first-
floor windows were vaulted, and the second-story windows
were embellished with wrought-iron balconies. There was a
red-brick church with a white spire, and several of the business buildings were built of brick. Some displayed decora-
tive white columns. Most of the stores were clapboard but
even these were whitewashed and had commodious double
doors, high windows, and elaborate false fronts with
scrolled tops screening the flat roofs. Slanted panoplies pro-
tected all the boardwalks in the business district from summer sun and winter snow. The porch of the Comstock
House offered rocking chairs on a broad porch and was a
favorite gathering place for substantial citizens.

The marshal had designed the jailhouse. It was built like
a fortress. The stone walls were a foot thick and the windows could be closed from the inside with heavy oak shut-
ters. This was true of the barred cell windows, except they
were fitted with iron staves that could be securely locked in
place. There were gun slots in the walls. The lockup was
built to withstand a siege, and no prisoner ever had escaped
from it.

The office, lighted by shiny bracket lamps, was comfortable. The walls were plastered and whitewashed. The marshal had his polished oak desk, unscarred by boot heels,
and a chair padded with a tawny-colored cushion. Bart's
chair was not pillowed. A pine gun cabinet behind the marshal's desk held four Winchester repeating rifles, and an ar-

senal could be stored in the closet next to it. When the weather permitted a fire, a fat-bellied cast-iron stove always held a fragrant pot of coffee.

Bart didn't think he'd snoozed but he started when he heard Fargo unlock and open the closet door. The marshal kept a jug of whiskey there and he sometimes brought it out on nights like this when the vigil would be tedious. The deputy's chair legs thumped to the planks and he pushed back his hat. "What're you doing?" he asked expectantly.

Fargo set the jug on the desk and hooked two tin cups from the drawer. "I'm half inclined to take a cup of whiskey back to the prisoners," he said mildly.

"With so few hours left to them, it'd be a waste," Bart objected strenuously. It was unthinkable the marshal should even consider giving whiskey to the prisoners but abruptly the suggestion provided Bart with the answer to Fargo's unnatural behavior throughout the evening. It was a strange solution, but knowing the marshal as he did, Bart was certain it was true. The marshal felt obligated to the Fiddler and his partners. He owed them and had to pay his debt before they died. It was that simple.

The badmen had made the marshal look good. Pinkerton's hadn't been able to corral them. Fargo had strolled into the Miners' Bank unaware while three of them were rifling the safe and they'd surrendered without firing a shot. The bank had been grateful and rewarded Fargo with a pouch containing twenty-five double eagles. Of course, Cyrus did not know the money had come from the bank, he had been at great pains to explain. His scruples about accepting so much as a glass of beer for performing his duty were well known. The pouch had mysteriously appeared one day in the drawer of his desk.

"Where else could it of come from?" Bart had asked.

"I have no idea," the marshal had said, feigning ignorance.

"If you don't know who left it there you can't give it back," Bart had observed.

"That's right," Fargo had agreed and flipped a double eagle to Bart. That had closed the matter.

Now the marshal sloshed whiskey in the cups and moved one toward the deputy. Bart did not reach for it. He was listening to the quiet. "When'd they stop a-fiddling and a-singing?" he asked, alarmed.

"They tuckered out," the marshal said placidly. "With what's facing them, I don't for the life of me see how they can sleep. I thought the whiskey might help. When they close their eyes, they're each alone and all they can see is the hangman's noose. You should be grateful they're quiet. You've been grousing all night about that fiddle."

"Cyrus!" Bart said sharply. "It's too damned quiet."

"Stop fretting, Bart," Fargo said wearily. "Have a snort. You're touchy. It's the weather. We've both been here right along and I haven't been asleep. Nobody's come in and nobody's gone out. We're snug and tight as always."

"No we ain't!" Bart was in a panic. "I don't hear them snoring or even breathing." He bolted for the cell block corridor without touching his whiskey.

The marshal snatched a lantern from a peg above his desk, and his long strides put him on Bart's heels. At the bars of the pen, the lantern puddled the three double-tiered bunks with murky light. Bart felt the marshal go rigid. The bunks were empty and no one was in the cell. Even the fiddle was gone. Two bars had been filed from the window while the strings were screeching. The birds had flown the coop.

II

That stifling, listless night the dust-laden air filled a man's throat but he couldn't gulp enough oxygen into his lungs to breathe. The town was filled with panting people. They'd come in from miles around for the hangings. Men had ridden down from the diggings and up from Carson City. Entire families had made the bone-rattling trip in wagons from nearby farms where the poor soil was grubbed for vegetables worth their weight in gold. There had been two cattle drives that day from ranches to the southeast in the Big Smoky Valley. The cows had sweated off a good many pounds but nobody gave a one-bit damn. The butcher shops and restaurants would pay any asking price and pass it on to the miners. The punchers should have ridden back before the dawn of another burning day but they'd stayed around to see the fun.

If the weather had been tolerable it would have been a gala evening. The people were there, on the street, but they weren't moving much. A man with any sense stayed put where he was. They were sitting on the hitchracks and on the edges of the boardwalks with their heels on the baked dirt, and on the porch at the Comstock House letting their weight tip the rocking chairs to stir up a little air without working for it. The saloons were busy but there was no violence in any of them. Men drooped at the bars, elbow to elbow, silently sipping their beers or whiskies. It was too hot to think, let alone to talk.

The batwings at the Full House saloon fluttered and four men drifted out. From their tall hats and high heels, they were cowpokes from one of the drives. They walked on lazy legs to the hitchrail for their ponies. At the rack they halted for a moment as if they'd been pulled up short by a long rope, and then four coarse voices blasted the torpid night with one word roared in unison:

"*Horsethief!*"

If it hadn't been for the heat that sucked up a man's juices, the pokes' outraged cry would have brought a crowd on the run. There was no critter meaner than a horsethief. As it was, a few men nearby dropped from the racks and left their places on the boardwalks. Two ambled over from the Comstock and half a dozen came out from the Full House. No more than a dozen gathered loosely in the patch of light about the pokes, looking dully at them and the vacant rail. They were spectators only and were not inclined to be involved.

"When'd they get took?" a bald-headed man in the white shirt and black vest of a shopkeeper finally inquired. He sounded more polite than interested.

One of the punchers, a burly, hard-eyed man with heavy reddish stubble on his jaw, yelped in anguish, "Ain't nobody going to do nothing about our ponies?"

"Get the marshal," suggested a lanky youth in sodbuster bib overalls.

Three of the group from the Full House returned to the saloon, but a fourth hesitated. He turned, peered down the street, and called, "He's coming now, the marshal is."

Those who hadn't left idled curiously another moment, waiting for the marshal and his deputy, who lagged a pace or two behind. Bart could not match Fargo's purposeful strides, which jolted his .44 and jounced the star on his chest. Bart was breathless, flushed and indignant at the jailbreak. He blamed Fargo but he hadn't told him so. The marshal was ferocious.

"Our ponies been stolen!" the husky cowboy yelled before Fargo and Bart reached the saloon's rack.

"How many?" Fargo's voice was honed steel, and under the broad brim of his white hat his face was a fearsome mask of frozen rage.

"Four paints," the poke answered when Fargo confronted him. He seemed subdued by the marshal's unexpected fury.

The first onlookers returned and others joined them, apparently sensing something explosive in the abrupt appearance of the marshal and his deputy.

"Four prisoners broke jail," Fargo announced in a voice so icy it even chilled Bart. "When we find them, we'll have the horsethieves."

"Them that was to hang?" someone called accusingly.

"The same," the marshal said bleakly.

The miners and the cowboys, the shopkeepers and the farmers who'd come to see the circus began to snarl. Fanned by the hot breath of those who repeated the news, word of the prisoners' escape spread like wind-whipped grass fire along the street. Before, they'd been inactive as individuals, but now this one and that one left his perch or seat and moved into angry groups. Together they no longer were their own selves but a gathering, inflamed crowd. Each man's voice became one with the common cry of many. Emotion trampled thought and reason in the vengeful clamor of the mob.

Bart saw the marshal struggle to maintain composure.

The deep lines about his mouth twisted and writhed and then his face contorted as he lost control. "Quiet!" he thundered in such black rage that those nearest fell back. "Who saw them leave?" When no voice lifted from the tight silence, he demanded, "A posse. Who'll go? Or do I deputize the town?"

"We'll go," one of the four punchers offered, "if you'll get us horses."

"Take the outlaws' horses," the marshal barked. "They're stabled in the livery barn. Who else?"

Volunteers for the posse surged forward—grim-faced, gun-toting men with resentment glittering in their slitted eyes.

"Good," the marshal said, voice still huge. "You men with horses at the racks here, climb up and meet us at the jailhouse." He spun and started down the middle of the street.

Bart was breathing more normally than Fargo now and trotted beside him. "Nobody seen them go," Bart puzzled aloud. "How'd they steal them ponies and ride off without being seen? How we know where to go to look, Cyrus?"

"Stop whining," Fargo said grimly. "There's only two ways they could have gone. Stage road, north or south. We'll get them, and when we do, they'll pay for this. That's the criminal for you. Do him a kindness and he kicks you in the teeth."

Bart understood the marshal's bitterness. He must be worrying about his reputation and wondering whether he'd be bound to return the reward money to the bank if the outlaws weren't recaptured. "They could of gone west into the mountains or east across the flats," he pointed out.

"Too rough one way, too open the other," Fargo said impatiently. "They'll hightail for Carson City and California." He laughed harshly. "They're counting on the start they've got. What they don't know is, those cow ponies been on a drive in this heat and are stove in. They won't last an hour, the way they'll haze them. We'll make them wish it was a peaceful hanging."

"Where'd they get the file, Cyrus?"

"That damned runt must have passed it through the bars," Fargo said savagely.

Riders were pounding by them in gritty swirls of dust, and a score of sweating men on snorting horses awaited orders when they reached the jailhouse. Clopping still sounded on the crusted street as more volunteers loped near.

"Get the horses," Fargo told Bart as he mounted the stoop to face the growing posse. He was haranguing the angry men when Bart rode his piebald from the stable behind the jail, leading the marshal's mustang. The marshal was shouting, "You know the four we're after. They'll be riding the paints they stole. I want those men alive."

"We'll shoot them on sight," a voice called gruffly, "so's they don't get away from you again."

"Hell no!" another voice boomed. "We come to see them strung up."

A third bellowed, "We'll hogtie them and drag them back on their yellow bellies."

"Order!" the marshal roared, and when the hubbub subsided, he said in heavy-hammer tones, "What I had in mind is, we take them alive, and when we do, we'll string them up on the spot, only we won't hang them by their necks. We'll hang them by their heels until the blood runs out of their ears and eyes and they gag to death on it."

The hurrah was like rolling thunder until a strident voice

overrode the din. "That's something the town ought to see."

Bart saw Fargo was listening to the rumbling wave of approval that responded to this last suggestion. The marshal swung into his saddle and called, "That's the way we'll do it, boys. Haul them back at ropes' ends. String them up by their heels at the courthouse. Give the town its money's worth. Let the country know how we treat badmen out here." Amid an outburst of cheers, he rode through the group, separating the riders into two parties of about fifteen men each. He flung his arm to the left. "Those over here ride with the deputy and take the road north." He motioned to his right. "You men come with me south." To all he proclaimed, "Good hunting!"

The riders peeled off in opposite directions, and the hoofbeats drummed a rolling cadence. A tawny veil of dust draped the street, curtaining the lights and making them glimmer. As distance muted the sound of the posse parties, the town settled back to wait. Men returned to the hitchracks and boardwalks. The rocking chairs creaked again on the Comstock porch. Customers shoved back into the sour heat of the saloons. It was no cooler than it had been earlier, but there was a difference: Everyone was talking now. The town was excited about the foot-hanging reprisal the marshal planned. That was the way to handle things. It was going to be a better show than they'd been promised.

III

In the luminescent sky, a full moon glowed on the hazed streets of Virginia City. The saloon lamps put dust halos on the men sitting on the rails and walks. Only the moonlight filtered on four figures prone behind the parapet on the flat roof of the jailhouse. They were motionless, chins resting on folded arms, and all were bareheaded.

The Fiddler rolled and propped himself on his elbow. For a moment he considered his companions in the milky moonlight.

Two-finger Jake looked like a Turkish brigand. His skull was hairless, skin oily and glistening, but his upper lip had nurtured a fiercely magnificent black mustache. It was thick and swept into twisted curls extending well beyond his cheeks. Hooded dark eyes were deep-set to a tomahawk nose, and his face was swarthy and long. He'd lost three fingers from his left hand when a cashier had slammed a safe door on them, and he'd cut them off with his Bowie knife to free himself. He was cheerless and lived a glum existence in a gloomy world but he had his own peculiar brand of courage.

Montana Mac was enormous. He was sometimes called the Bear and, haired-over as he was, he looked as if he might just have lumbered down from the forested heights. Only two amber eyes, large and gentle as a deer's, the pink ball of a nose, and fat red lips suggested that the black brush of tangled hair and beard concealed a man. Usually he was amiable but he could be a grizzly when circumstances demanded ferocity and tenacity. He'd spent an entire winter in Wyoming Territory's Wind River mountains tracking down a renegade band of Arapahos who'd murdered his trapping partner and left him afoot.

The Carson Kid was a go-to-hell-on-a-bucking-horse sort of fellow who had a wild streak that often was very funny— like the time he'd knotted an eagle feather in his hair, daubed his cheeks and chest with black and white slashes, and robbed a bank alone wearing half a dozen trimmed-down beaver pelts that looked like scalps on his beaded belt. Some dark spirit inhabited the Kid's slight frame of bone and skin. Normally jaunty and quick to quip, he could be a hotspur who erupted into violence. The Fiddler did his damndest to get along with him and keep peace within the band.

With the sage and placid Preacher, who had survived twice the Fiddler's twenty-five years, they were an unlikely crew.

The Kid squirmed to a crouch and rapped the Fiddler's forearm as the rumbling of the bunched horses faded. "We did it!" he said jubilantly.

When Mac sat up, he humped to keep his head below the wall. "The marshal was techy as a mountain cat with his paw in a trap," he said cheerfully.

"That crowd was downright hostile," growled Jake, getting to his knees.

"They felt cheated," the Fiddler observed. There was a sadness in him he had not known before. The people hadn't come to see justice done. They'd come to see men tortured.

"We ain't out of this by a damn sight," Jake reminded them. "We'd best make tracks."

"Can't keep the Preacher waiting," the Kid said lightly.

The Fiddler, bow and fiddle in his left hand, started to crawl toward the rear of the building, and the others followed.

"That lawdog was mad 'nough to eat the devil with his horns on," Mac said happily, moving awkwardly behind the others.

"Save your breath for running," Jake advised.

Although sobered by the blood-craze of the crowd, the Fiddler was pleased with their successful break. The plan had worked just as he'd known it would when he'd outlined it to the Preacher months before in the private sitting room at Millie the Madam's parlor house in Cheyenne.

"We've been lucky so far," he'd told the Preacher, glancing appreciatively at the elegant furniture, the rose-festooned wallpaper, and the drawn red velvet drapes that insulated them from the howling Wyoming wind and prying eyes. He'd selected Millie's private quarters for the conference because here he felt secure. No one entered her apartment without an invitation.

"It's not been chance, Frank," the Preacher said quietly. He was wearing a black string tie and black frock coat. Sitting stiffly upright on the small horsehair sofa, he looked austere. "It's been your genius for planning that has enabled us to make the raids and safe getaways. Who would suspect a robbery was in progress with all attention diverted by your fiddling on the street?"

Millie came into the room carrying a tray with a silver tea service, dainty china cups decorated with forget-me-nots and a plate of cakes. She was a robust redhead but she bore herself with gentility. She placed the tray on a marble-topped table, sat primly in a needlepoint chair beside it, and poured. "Franklyn has many talents," she commented. Her enunciation was meticulous. Rumor suggested she was the daughter of a priest and had been educated in the East. "I've always felt he should have matriculated at the conservatory."

"Yes, madam, meaning no offense," the Preacher agreed. He accepted a cup of tea, manipulating the saucer adroitly in his crippled hand. "We weren't nearly so successful until Frank came along."

"I didn't come along," the Fiddler said emphatically. "Jake and Mac and the Kid came along and saved me when that posse at Tucson was about to run me down."

"It was their duty to rescue you," the Preacher reminded him. "They had pulled that heist, and you had no part in it nor knowledge of it. Those upright citizens were ready to place the blame on you simply because you were a stranger." He plucked a tart from the plate Millie offered and thanked her with a gracious smile. "However that may be, you were under no obligation to cast your lot with us. You were free to go your way."

"I never thought I'd become an outlaw," the Fiddler said, holding his cup to Millie to be refilled. "I enjoyed the unencumbered, random life the four of you were leading and I don't like banks and railroads. They're taking the country away from the people."

"The concept you offered stunned all of us," the Preacher said. "You to draw the crowd while the others proceeded in comparative safety at their leisure!"

"That idea took no special faculty," the Fiddler objected. "It was an excuse for not participating in the actual stickup. I'd never point a gun at a man unless I was going to shoot him. In its way, it's similar to the role you play.

You are the harmless little man who cases the jobs, and an innocent bystander when the raid is made."

"It's an ideal arrangement," the Preacher conceded. "Each of us performs the task for which he is best suited."

Millie laughed discreetly. "You're both such *gentlemen* for your profession."

"I return the compliment, madam," the Preacher said gallantly. "You are a lady."

"Thank you," Millie said, blushing delicately.

"Now, as I started to say, we've been fortunate," the Fiddler returned to the reason for the meeting. "It is inevitable the day will come when we'll be caught. We should formulate a contingency plan against such an emergency."

"You are so clever, Franklyn," Millie said quietly. "What did you say your surname is?"

"Bye. Franklyn Bye."

"Yes, Dye," she misinterpreted. "There are Dyes in Boston. A genteel family. Are you related to the Boston Dyes?"

"Not to my knowledge," the Fiddler said.

"You were saying . . ." the Preacher prompted.

"Yes." The Fiddler smiled at Millie and declined more tea. "If there is a run-in with the law and my complicity is not suspected, I shall make it known so I can be taken into custody with Jake, Mac, and the Kid."

"But that would be foolhardy, Frank," the Preacher declared. "Do you want me to confess my part as well?"

"No," the Fiddler said. "It is essential you remain at liberty. There is one provision to this plan. If the law interrupts us at our work, there is to be no gunplay, no shootout."

"What is the plan, Frank?" the Preacher asked, withdrawing.

"Simply this. In the event we are apprehended, I shall contrive to leave my fiddle behind. It will not be noticed in the excitement of the arrest or surrender. Pick it up and spirit it away. I have removed the fingerboard, drilled a groove, and inserted a hard steel file. The slot is concealed with a thin layer of blackened resin. If I hold onto the fiddle when we are taken or I surrender, there is the possibility they might not allow me to keep it. At the last moment, you bring it to me at the jail with some plausible story and make suitable arrangements for a getaway and hideout. We'll break out. You can judge where to rendezvous by the circumstances."

"Splendid," the Preacher said and beamed.

Millie gasped softly. "It is inspired. I never should have thought of anything so clever. You and your associates are welcome to come here. My guests would be delighted to hear you perform again. Wherever you have entertained, you have been highly regarded."

"Thank you, Millie," the Fiddler had said sincerely.

Now, many days' distance from safe haven at Millie's parlor house, the Fiddler wondered what sort of hideout the Preacher had obtained. The getaway horses were at hand, he knew. The enraged cry of "Horsethief!" had reached the jailhouse roof. He dropped from the edge to the stable and from it into the alleys that ran behind and beside the lockup. The Kid, Jake, and Mac landed near him and they all hugged the stable wall, looking up and down the moonlighted passageways for the Preacher and the ponies.

"I don't see or hear nothing, friend," the Kid said nervously.

"Maybe he don't know where to look for us," Jake growled.

"He'll be along," the Fiddler said confidently. "We covered this part of it."

"I'd feel better if we had hats," Jake grumbled. "The moon lights my noggin like a lantern."

"I feel skinned without a gun," Mac said. "I want my .44. After the way them skunks mean-mouthed us, I ain't about to be took if we're cornered."

The nicker of a horse was cut short, as if someone had pinched its nostrils. The Preacher came around the blind corner of the alley, dwarfed by the four paints he was leading.

"Evening, Preacher," the Fiddler said, grinning. He stepped away from the stable. "How did you manage rustling those ponies under the whole town's fat nose?"

The Preacher brought the paints to the stable. "It was nothing," he said modestly. "I didn't take them all at once. I'd ride them off, one at a time, slumped in the saddle like I was carrying a load of redeye. Nobody gave a second look."

"You'll be quite a man if you ever grow up," the Kid quipped.

The Fiddler noticed that for the first time since he'd known the Preacher, he was wearing a gunbelt. He'd been prepared to make a stand if necessary. The Fiddler reached for the bridle of the near pony.

The Preacher held back. "No. We'll leave these stolen horses hitched in the marshal's stable."

"That's amusing," the Fiddler said and laughed, "but they'll be discovered by morning, and the marshal will know that we're afoot."

"Precisely." The Preacher smacked his lips with apparent satisfaction. "The posse will come back empty-handed and mean-tempered. When they discover these ponies and have no reports of others missing, they'll think you've holed up, and they'll tear the town apart looking for you. It will give us time to get settled. I have my roan and some horses of a sort hidden in the brush."

"I do admire the way you think," the Fiddler said. "Maybe we can take care of two other items while you're putting up the ponies. Is there a storage closet in the marshal's office?"

The Preacher was silent for a thoughtful moment. "Yes," he recalled. "I noticed a door. Behind the marshal's desk, next to the gun cabinet."

"I'm going to have a look," the Fiddler said. He handed the violin and bow to the Kid. "Maybe the old hangman stashed our guns and hats in there."

"Should you risk it, Frank?" the Preacher asked cautiously.

"Should you have chanced stealing horses on Main Street?" the Fiddler chided and added with a grin, "What addle-brain would be watching an empty jail?"

Although he'd dismissed the Preacher's warning carelessly, the Fiddler was aware of the danger with the entire town on Main Street and inflamed by the jailbreak. When he left the alley, he crawled along the front of the lockup close to the wall, searching the street for passersby. The nearest person he could see was a boardwalk-sitter a block away, and he was looking in the other direction. The Fiddler kept to the floor in the lamp-lighted office and sat on the floor behind the marshal's desk facing the closet. The closet door was locked as he'd expected and he had no tool to pry it open. He got to his knees quickly, put his shoulder against the wall, grasped the knob, and heard heels rapping the boards just outside. He fell behind the desk. The stroller paused at the open front door. The

Fiddler braced his foot against the desk, ready to spring if the man grew curious and entered. After a moment the heels clattered away. When the Fiddler could no longer hear the bootfalls, he crawled to the door, scanned the street, and found a man crossing to the Full House. The Fiddler was perspiring more freely than he had been.

He climbed to his heels, ran to the closet, braced himself, and yanked the knob mightily. The lock plate yielded at his first tug. At the second, the metal ripped from the door frame. The hats were two-deep in stacks on a shelf, the gunbelts on pegs. He swept everything to the floor, ignoring the whiskey jug, although he felt the need for a jolt. He pushed the desk chair against the door to hold it in place and dropped to his knees with his .44 in his hand.

When there was no outcry, no racket from running men, he buckled on his gunbelt and crawled from the marshal's office with the other three belts encircling his right arm. The hats were heaped in his left. He searched the street and walks. No one seemed to have moved. He snaked into the alley and ran to the stable where the others were hiding. Jake, Mac, and the Kid claimed their guns and hats from his arms and he slapped his own tawny-colored Stetson on his head and laughed.

"There will be turmoil and tumult when the marshal discovers you paid a visit during his absence to reclaim your weapons," the Preacher predicted.

"There will be hell to pay," the Fiddler agreed and chuckled. "I hope the hideout is secure."

"If you don't stop flapping your lips, they'll be back before we're started," Jake said.

The Preacher led the way up the dingy alley to the west where flimsy miners' shacks squatted empty and dark on either side. The confined heat rose from the littered dirt in

layers that smelled of garbage and offal and gagged the
Fiddler. He was ready to forsake the conveniences of town
life and return to the open.

One cabin some distance up the hill showed a lamp, and
the file approached warily. They were some ten yards from
it when a massive black dog charged through the open
door, snarling and lunging toward them. The dog's eyes
were fiery in the creamy light, its fangs were bared, and the
neck hairs bristled. The men halted, waiting tensely, and
the Fiddler slipped the Bowie knife from his gunbelt.

A hulking man in a nightshirt appeared in the doorway.
"Wassa madder, Gus?" he bawled. He swayed and braced
himself against the door frame. "Gotta Shinem'n? 'll git m'
gun."

Beside the Fiddler, the Kid stiffened and drew his Colt.
Eyes intent on the dog, growling low in its throat, the
Fiddler felt the motion and slammed the .44 back in the
Kid's holster. The dog stalked closer, ready to spring. The
Preacher squatted and held out his hand. The animal
turned its attention to him but seemed less threatening.
The Preacher, still squatting, hurled an object far up the
alley. The dog bounded after it, racing past the shack as
the tipsy man returned to the doorway carrying a scatter
gun.

"Chasin' tail," the man muttered and then shouted,
"Go git 'er." He stumbled back inside.

"Bone?" the Fiddler asked the Preacher in a whisper.

"With lots of meat," the Preacher said quietly and
chuckled. "My own contingency plan. I expected something like this."

They waited a few moments and then slipped through
the path of light outside the cabin. Fifteen paces beyond,

the dog was gnawing the bone. He did not desert it, only growling at each man as they passed.

The Kid slipped up beside the Fiddler. "Look, friend," he said between clenched teeth, "don't you ever touch my gun hand again."

"A shot would have exploded the townspeople into their saddles," the Fiddler told him.

"For whatever reason, friend, don't touch me when my gun is out," the Kid warned and dropped back.

They climbed for ten minutes beyond the last deserted shack with a sagging roof and tilted walls. They all were breathing heavily and popping sweat when the Preacher halted near a stand of single-leaf piñon and juniper bushes. It was no cooler near the hilltop but the air was clear. Below, the main street lay like a jeweled ribbon, lights glittering through the dust-mist and shimmering red, yellow, and blue.

"How much farther?" the Fiddler asked. He was beginning to worry about the time they were spending.

"We're here," the Preacher said with a smile. "They're tethered in there, deep." He plunged into the tangled clump.

The Fiddler was not often astonished but he gaped in complete disbelief at the five shadowed horse-shapes the Preacher showed them. There was the Preacher's own roan and two mustangs that appeared sound enough but the other two horses were spavined farm plugs. They were slab-sided and shad-bellied and their heads were bowed with age. They were neither saddled nor bridled, just a played-out work team with rope halters around their noses.

"What the hell is this supposed to mean?" the Fiddler demanded angrily.

"They'll get us there," the Preacher said calmly.

"Hey friend, you mean two of us is supposed to ride them?" the Kid said shrilly.

"Them two old nags is dead but they just won't lay down," Mac observed.

"If our trail is cut, we can't make a run for it," the Fiddler said tightly. "We'll have to shoot it out."

"We should of kept the paints and made for the Sierras," Jake said.

The Preacher was not ruffled. "If the posses circle back, they'd have crossed our path that way," he said. "Even with this wagon team, we can be securely hidden within the hour if we don't dally."

"I don't like this," the Fiddler said. He was not annoyed, but he was profoundly disturbed.

"Who gets to ride the saddle horses?" the Kid demanded.

"The Preacher rides his roan," the Fiddler said. "Regardless of what a man's done, he gets to keep his horse." He turned to the little man. "Make us four sticks. The two short sticks ride the plugs."

Jake and Mac drew the work horses. It had been fair and they didn't complain but their eyes were flat as they untied the halter ropes from the scrub pine.

"Watch it now, friends, don't let them broncs throw you," the Kid jibed.

The Fiddler handed him the fiddle and bow, made a stirrup of his hands, and helped Mac straddle the broad back of one work horse. Jake made the ascent unassisted.

The Preacher swung a leg onto the roan, and the others followed him on a faint trail that wandered north through the brush. They rode in gloomy silence. Below, north and south of the twinkling town, the stage road was feathered where the two search parties had kicked up dust. The

Fiddler kept looking ahead and behind along the road for signs of the returning riders.

"Is it far?" he finally called to the Preacher.

"No more than six miles," the Preacher said quietly.

"That close!" the Fiddler exclaimed, further alarmed. Tomorrow, after the posses had searched the town, they'd fan out and start to beat the brush and rummage through the nearby ranches and farms. "Is it safe?"

"You shouldn't have to ask that, Frank," the Preacher said reproachfully. "It's the best hideout a man could ask."

The Fiddler was moodily thoughtful. It was a bad getaway and there were no good hideouts. At best any refuge was a touchy thing. If you had to go into hiding and stay there and rely on someone else to be your eyes and ears, you quickly became suspicious of what you were told and uneasy for fear you'd be taken unaware. The days and nights were filled with anxiety, and every sound was suspect. Cabin fever was no ailment compared with hideout sickness, and when the confinement was prolonged, it was intolerable. Brooding put misery in a man's soul and filled his mind with doubts about himself. If others were with him, they gave him no comfort but shared only their despair.

"What is this hideout?" the Fiddler asked uneasily. "A ranch, abandoned mine, some hole in the hills?"

"A ranch," the Preacher answered without turning his head.

"It must be a damned poor one," the Fiddler said.

"It is poor," the Preacher said evenly, "but it suits our purpose."

A poverty-stricken rancher willing to risk his neck for a few dollars would also be willing to sell them out for a reward. "How did you hear about this place?" the Fiddler

asked suspiciously. "Does this rancher make a practise of
hiding men on the run? If others know about it, word may
have reached the marshal."

"We're the first," the Preacher said shortly. "The marshal has no reason for suspicion."

"If we're the first he's taken in, you must have been very
persuasive," the Fiddler observed dryly.

"Not particularly," the Preacher said.

"You're in this with us, you know," the Fiddler reminded him. "You won't be able to move around the way
you have."

"I know," the Preacher said sharply. After a moment, he
added more patiently, "During the past days, I made what
personal purchases we'd require. The rancher will buy the
less obvious necessities as the need arises."

"It's too bad you can't circulate the way you always
have," the Fiddler said. "We need a listening post."

"The rancher will go to town from time to time and let
us know what is happening," the Preacher said.

"This is an unusually co-operative rancher," the Fiddler
remarked. He completely distrusted the hideout and the
rancher. "What did you have to pay?"

"One hundred dollars."

"That's chicken feed!" The Fiddler's concern was grave.
No man should value his life so cheaply. "For how long?"

"For however long we have to stay," the Preacher said.
"We're providing our own sustenance."

The Fiddler studied the Preacher's back. With his
stunted stature, he did not sit tall in the saddle but he sat
straight and his shoulders were squared. He was defiant,
the Fiddler decided. He realized the arrangements he'd
made were unacceptable. From time to time, the Fiddler
heard a growl of protest from Jake or Mac well behind on

the heavy-footed team. The Kid, too, knew that the Preacher had blundered. Usually quick with a flippant remark, he'd been tight-lipped on this ride.

"I'll mention just one more thing," the Fiddler told the Preacher. "I hope this hideout of yours isn't a hayloft where we'll swelter and sneeze."

It wasn't a direct question, and the Preacher dodged a direct comment. He said, "You'll be more comfortable than anyone in town."

The trail squeezed into a lofty stand of pine and thick black shadows. The ground was carpeted with needles, and the group moved silently. They wound through the trees for about half an hour before they broke into the open again and pushed on across barren hillside until the dragging pace and fleeting minutes made the Fiddler nervous. "How far now?" he called.

The Preacher transferred the reins to the fingers of his shriveled arm and pointed across a gulley to the top of a steep slope. "Yonder," he said.

Although the Fiddler could not see what lay beyond the high edge, it looked as if it would be a barren and unfriendly ledge with little cover. They dipped through the dry gulch, and the horses pawed up an incline of layered stone to a grassy bench below a billowing range of hills. Beside a lone ponderosa pine, a whitewashed clapboard house gleamed with silver sheen in the moonlight. The mighty tree stood like a tall sentinel commanding an uninterrupted sweep of the countryside. Several miles away and far below, the stage road lay like a scar upon the land. There was dust hanging above it but no riders were in sight.

The house was trim enough but small. It could not contain more than two rooms. A porch shadowed the front and there were no lamps burning inside. The Fiddler could see no one but he thought he heard the creak of a rocking chair. What appeared to be a well-tended garden with two long rows of stunted corn lay between the house and a thimble-sized stick corral. Snugged into the protective bosom of a swelling hill, a little white barn huddled as if for shelter from winter storms. The barn had a pitched roof to shed snow. There could not be more than five stalls, the Fiddler thought, and scarce room in the cramped loft to bed five men.

The Preacher led them past a wooden-boxed pump and water trough straight to the open double-doors of the barn. A black and white dog that seemed to know the Preacher trotted up with feathery tail waving and greeted him with a friendly whoof, then sniffed the rest of them as they climbed down. Jake, Mac, and the Kid were looking cold-eyed at the Preacher.

"The three of you," he told them, "take the horses to pasture behind the corral after we unsaddle. There's a stream they'll find. I'm going to take Frank to the house to meet the rancher. We'll meet you back here at the barn."

"I'll unsaddle the horses," the Kid muttered to the Fiddler. "Go up there with him and learn the worst."

It was a paltry, impossible hideout, the Fiddler thought, looking up at the loft space. Searchers would immediately go through the hay with pitchforks. He held his fiddle and bow in his left hand, and his right rested on the butt of his gun as he followed the Preacher to the house. They could not stay here, not even this night. In the small hours when the saddle-wearied posses were bedded, they'd have to rustle horses and saddles and take their chances on the run. Precious time wasted already and their lives were at stake.

The Fiddler heard the chair stop rocking as the Preacher and he stepped onto the porch. Someone came toward them from the far deep shadows, walking quickly and lightly like a young man. The Fiddler was further dismayed. He'd hoped at the least to find some experience and wisdom here, some help to start them on their way, some knowledge about the mountains. The slight, lithe figure in Levi's and shirt came to meet them with extended hand.

"This is the rancher," the Preacher introduced. "My niece, known hereabouts as the Widow Carrington."

IV

"The name is Boothe, or Boots, if you prefer," the Preacher's niece said, shaking the Fiddler's hand. "So you're the Fiddler."

Surprisingly, the way she frankly took his measure did not make him feel uncomfortable. The Preacher apparently had told her about him and she was openly curious. He returned the appraisal. Although slim-hipped in tight Levi's, she was not nearly so slight as he'd thought at first. Under a man's washed-pale work shirt, much too large for her, full breasts looked firm in profile. Her dark hair was short-cropped and a saucy elf-lock clung to her moist forehead. She looked like an urchin with gamin eyes that were mischievous when she smiled. Boots was good to look at and as a woman he liked her. As a rancher to hide them out and turn away an infuriated marshal and vengeful posse, he rejected her completely. Even if the ranch had offered suitable shelter, he was aghast that the Preacher would expose her to the perils of such a situation.

"We're beholden," he said to her. "It's a chancy thing, aiding us with a posse on our heels."

"I needed the money," she said forthrightly. Her voice was pleasantly low and musical. "I'd have done it anyway. I've always done what Milford said to do, ever since I was a child."

"Milford?" the Fiddler questioned.

"Uncle Milford." She laughed, a good laugh of genuine amusement. "You call him the Preacher. He was one, you know, back home in Illinois."

"Now, Boots!" The Preacher sounded vexed. "You've lived here long enough to know a man is accepted at face value and his past isn't held against him."

"Milford," she said severely but an impish twinkle was in her eyes. "It's the other way around. I don't care what you are now but you were a good preacher until that Chicago congregation turned you down because of your appearance and you went sour on Christianity."

The Fiddler brushed aside a hank of golden hair that had tumbled over an eye when he'd removed his hat, and he laughed. "He still can be very convincing. We do appreciate your hospitality. We won't compromise you long. A few hours tonight, only until we can round up some horses and ride on."

"But Milford said you'd be staying on." She sounded disappointed. "I was looking forward to hearing you play."

"We agreed," the Preacher said sonorously, sounding as if he had the authority of the pulpit behind him, "that we'd remain in hiding until the law decided that we'd slipped out of the state."

"No complaints, Boots, nothing but gratitude," the Fiddler told her. "It's safe enough here tonight but they're bound to start searching the farms and ranches. I assume you meant to hide us in the barn."

"Yes, the barn," the Preacher interjected. He was smiling.

"It's no good," the Fiddler said flatly. "It's the first place they'll look."

"Doesn't he know?" Boots asked her uncle. She sounded amused.

"I didn't tell him," the Preacher said. "He was so busy asking questions he wouldn't listen."

"If that's all," she told the Fiddler, "you'll be here long enough to play the violin for me many times."

Perhaps there was a root cellar beneath the house. "No," he said. "It would endanger you."

She looked at him quizzically, serious for a moment. "That's nice, Frank," she murmured and then she laughed. "You won't be in danger. I won't be in danger. Let's show him, Milford."

Jake, Mac, and the Kid were hunkered outside the barn, building cigarettes and not talking. They stood when they saw Boots. The Preacher introduced her only as the Widow Carrington and did not mention she was his niece. Jake and Mac touched their hats and mumbled acknowledgments.

The Kid, that *caballero*, swept off his hat with a flourish and his smile gleamed. "A pleasure, ma'am," he said, voice resonant and sincere to the ear.

"Howdy, boys," she said cheerfully and stepped into the barn with the Preacher.

So it was to be the loft. the Fiddler thought. She and the Preacher were taking this too lightly. He could understand Boots' naïveté. The Preacher confounded him. Did he expect her obvious innocence to turn away an embittered and determined marshal?

The Preacher lifted a lantern from a nail in a post. It flared yellow and smoked when he lighted it but he turned it down until the wick showed a steady, bright flame. The Fiddler saw it was a six-stall barn. All were empty and the barn smelled clean.

"Bring the saddles," the Preacher said and started for

the rear where slats nailed to the studs made a ladder to the mow.

"We can't take the lantern up there in the hay," the Fiddler objected, "and we won't need the saddles for our heads."

Boots teased him with a smile as she went with the Preacher into the left-hand stall at the back of the barn. It was a double stall and the feedbox was mounted on the rear wall. The Preacher handed the lantern to the Kid and gripped the top of the bin with his good right hand. "Put yourself to this," he told Mac.

The bearlike man closed his paws on the box, and the Fiddler looked to the ceiling, expecting to find a trapdoor.

"Now lift," the Preacher told Mac.

Mac looked puzzled but he did as he was told. Slowly the heavy feedbox section of the wall slid up until it was two feet off the floor. A draft of cold air gushed out. The Kid squatted quickly, holding the lantern into the opening. "Ho, friends!" he cried. "We have a cave in here."

Jake dropped beside the Kid, and the Fiddler stared at the Preacher and Boots. The Fiddler's amazement must have been apparent because she laughed. The hideout would be secure and unsuspected, but why would anyone build a barn against a hill to conceal a cave?

"You can let go," the Preacher told Mac, who still was gripping the box. "Once it's up, I can manage. Now, inside, all of you. We'll be safe. Kid, go ahead with the lantern."

The Kid crawled under the section, and Jake and Mac followed with the saddles.

"Go on," the Preacher urged the Fiddler. "I'll let it drop from the other side."

"I'll fork the hay around," Boots said. "I think you'll like it here, Frank. Tomorrow morning, if there's no one on the road, I'll rap the wall three times and you can come out for air."

The Fiddler's mind was turbulent. What possible reason could Boots have had for this hidden refuge? He smiled faintly, shook his head apologetically, and pushed his fiddle and bow ahead as he bellied under the sliding wall. He'd expected a small, confining cave but found he was in a short tunnel, and after a few yards the lantern ahead showed a passageway where the Kid, Jake, and Mac were walking erect. It was about three feet wide, hewn through gray stone. Behind, the panel thumped to the floor and in a moment the Preacher was with him.

"What is this, an old diggings?" the Fiddler asked.

"You'll see," the Preacher said and chuckled.

"Maybe her husband used it for something," Fiddler guessed. "Did he hide something in here?"

"That is a mystery," the Preacher said. "Perhaps you'll have some theory when you see the rest."

Ahead the lantern no longer illuminated the tunnel but was within a cavern. The men ahead had stopped and there was no sound from them. They were looking at a chamber so large the far wall receded into shadow. The Preacher pushed past and in a moment another lantern flared on a rough plank table at the far side. The Preacher raised the light above his head, and the Kid lifted his. The cavern was circular, about fifty feet in diameter, and the ceiling was about thirty feet high. It was not entirely natural but had been hand-hewn to its proportions. Ancient adzelike tools had left their scars on the gray stone. Some kind of prehistoric shrine or council chamber, the Fiddler concluded, discovering a blackened hollow that appeared to be a fire pit at the center of the floor. He glanced upward and found age-old smoke tracery on the ceiling.

There was not the expected silence of a cave and now his ears detected the gurgling sound of running water. He found the dark path that marked its course against the wall to his right.

"Come on over and make yourselves at home," the Preacher called and his voice echoed hollowly. He was pleased with himself.

The four walked across the cave in silence. The others were as awed as he, the Fiddler thought. When the Kid placed his lantern beside the Preacher's, their light showed two planks supported on cartridge cases to form a rough table. Other cases had been placed around it to serve as benches. A good store of supplies, provisions, and equipment was stacked against the walls and there was a pile of red blankets and two new California saddles. The Fiddler took swift inventory of the pots and pans, flour and coffee, meat and vegetables, tobacco, alarm clock, and personal items such as razors, mirror, soap, and towels. He was afraid the Preacher had left a back trail.

"How'd you manage all this?" he asked. "The store-keeper is sure to remember you, and the marshal will know we're holed up."

"He certainly would if I'd bought it all at one place in Virginia City," the Preacher agreed. "I borrowed Boots' wagon and drove to Carson City. I spread it out over three stores."

The Fiddler lifted the lid of a kettle and found potatoes, carrots, onions, and chunks of raw meat in water.

"For son-of-a-bitch stew tomorrow," the Preacher explained. He was smiling and it was plain he was enjoying himself. "I'll get it started soon. Boots can't risk feeding us. She offered to but I said no. When they come snooping around, she can't have enough on the range to feed a roundup crew."

"You've laid in enough of everything for us to eat like kings for a month," the Fiddler said cautiously, "but I don't think we should cook. We can eat cold. The smell of onions, bacon, coffee, mainly wood smoke, would seep under the feedbox."

"Nope," the Preacher said promptly. "Not if we hang up a wet blanket. I hammered in some nails and tried it out on Boots. It takes up the smell. Main problem with a wood fire is the fuel supply if we're pinned down here for long and can't get out. I made some fat lamps." He reached into a box and brought out a large tin filled with tallow and a broad wick. "Half a dozen, with iron racks to hold pots and pans. They'll do for all we need, even simmer stew if we leave it long enough."

Abruptly Mac laughed, a rumbling belly laugh. "We're loaded for bear," he said and dropped the two saddles he'd been carrying. He straddled one of the cartridge cases. "Let's get some vittles started. That jail grub knotted my gut."

Jake lowered his saddle and hauled up a case. The Kid teetered on a third.

"Who knows about this cave?" the Fiddler asked warily, still standing, but he laid his fiddle and bow on the table.

"Nobody," the Preacher said and lit a fat lamp. "It was Eli's secret. That was her husband. Even Boots had forgotten and nobody else ever knew."

The Fiddler looked at the Preacher curiously. That was a peculiar statement. If Boots had forgotten, then the Preacher must have reminded her. "Did you know her husband?" he asked.

"Yes, I knew Eli," the Preacher said. "A good many years ago."

"Was wondering how you knew where to come," Jake said, tossing his hat onto the pile of blankets. Light from the lanterns and lamp reflected on his head. "This place looks safe but I don't like the idea of being buried. It's like being in your grave."

"Friend," the Kid said, "the Preacher put you in your grave to keep you alive."

"Boots is young to be a widow," the Fiddler said. "What did Eli die from?"

The Preacher put the stew kettle on the rack over the fat lamp. "Bullet in the back."

"Why?" the Fiddler asked.

The Preacher looked at him a moment before he answered and briefly his eyes seemed vague and distant. "Who knows? He had no enemies, few friends. He was a close-mouthed, hard-working, honest poor man. He had nothing. This land is worthless."

"Maybe somebody wanted the widow," the Kid suggested.

"If he did, he hasn't been around to claim her," the Preacher said. "She runs this place by herself. Works like a man."

"She don't fool me, friend, for all that man haircut and clothes," the Kid said. "I know there's a woman inside. Maybe I put my brand on her."

The Preacher turned a stern face and baleful eye on the Kid. The Fiddler moved in quickly. "We've got to have some regulations and now's as good a time as any to get at them," he said. "We're all in the same wagon and what one of us does affects all of us. The little thing we overlook will be our last mistake. Boots said she'd signal when it was safe to go out. We won't leave at any time for any reason until we get that signal. There'll always be a lookout and we stay together." He glanced at the Preacher and grinned. "You did it proud all the way. There's not a thing you've overlooked."

"Well, maybe one thing you could of done," Jake muttered.

"I know what you're thinking, Jake," the Preacher said. He reached under the table and brought up a gray gallon crock. "You boys been in the hoosegow long enough to build up a thirst."

Mac pulled the beard away from his lips with the forefingers of both hands. "Don't do no vittles till the stew's done tomorrow," he said happily.

The Preacher lined up five tin cups, ran them full, and passed them around. The Fiddler pulled up a cartridge case. "I can use a belt," he said, and lifted his cup to the Preacher. After two good swallows that started some warmth in his gut, he said, "Preacher, you put your roan out with Boots' mustangs. When that posse gets here they're going to see an extra horse with a different brand."

"Nobody knows about her horses except she doesn't have enough to steal," the Preacher said. "I put a running iron to the roan. She wore a Cut and Slash brand. I ran those lines down to make a Diamond and burned a C in it. That's Boots' brand, the Diamond C."

"Preacher, you're slippery as sowbelly," Mac said.

"Hey friend," the Kid said to the Fiddler, "you talk too much. Don't have more rules, don't ask more questions tonight. We busted out and got here safe. Let's celebrate."

The Fiddler built a smoke. "Sure Kid, you're right. Let's keep it that way."

Jake worked at his whiskey. He was silent and morose.

"What's eating you?" the Preacher asked him.

"The four of us was cooped up long enough together so we're all talked out," he said. "Now here we are again with nothing to say or do."

"Damnit, find something to do," the Fiddler said, sensing the pressures building. "Wash your socks and shirt, clean your boots, scrub your head."

"Some poker?" the Preacher suggested.

The Kid brightened. "You brought cards? Hell, yes."

"We got no money," Jake mentioned. "That damned marshal grabbed everything we had. Seven double eagles I'd been stashing for a game. There's no point in poker if there's no stakes."

"Put it on the books," the Fiddler said. "The Preacher can keep tabs. Settle the accounts when we're out and make a hit." His normal good nature returned and he added, "If we're holed up long enough, someone's likely to walk away so rich he can afford to go straight."

"It's better'n just sitting like toads on a stump," Mac said.

The Preacher provided a rack of chips and broke open a deck of diamond-back cards. The Fiddler picked up an old saddle and two blankets. "Aren't you in, Frank?" the Preacher asked.

"I'm going to drape that soaked blanket over the feedbox and roll up," the Fiddler said. When he had his head on the saddle, he turned his face from the lanterns. The players were cutting for the deal.

He was tired enough so his bones did not feel the hard stone floor through the doubled blanket he'd used as a pad, but he was not particularly sleepy. He wanted to be alone and he wanted to think. The outcry of the crowd that had come to see the hangings troubled him considerably. He and the band were thieves and he'd never tried to justify their activities nor rationalize. Although he'd never used anything more lethal than a fiddle bow, they were outlaws who preyed upon society. But they were not killers; those in the crowd were.

The mania of the law-abiding citizens on the street that night had frightened him. He hadn't known people were like that. It wasn't an emotional fear for himself. Not a fright of being hanged, just like a man didn't let a fear of being shot and killed ride him. He was frightened of what those people were doing to themselves and to each other. The crowd was the cowardly killer who lusted for blood in a poverty of courage. Those people had wanted to witness the awesome spectacle of death without dirtying their hands or risking their precious hides. He'd seen man stripped to his feral nature and it appalled him.

He was a tranquil person and did not like such melancholy thoughts but he knew this confrontation with elemental man would profoundly affect the trail he rode henceforth. He was unsure which direction he'd take. He'd either pillage the community of man relentlessly because he no longer had tolerance or he'd hang up his gunbelt forever.

V

It was unnaturally quiet when the Fiddler awakened, and he lifted his head from the saddle, for the moment alarmed. A campfire burned near the stream, which he could hear, but there were none of the accustomed small sounds of the night. He smelled simmering stew and heard an alarm clock ticking and snoring men nearby and he sat up laughing quietly and thinking of Boots. His partners must have moved the fat lamp and turned down the lanterns when they finished their game.

He was alert and rested and so judged the time to be about five o'clock. When he'd pulled on his pants and boots, he went to the table, found a lantern, and put a lucifer to the wick, shielding the light from the sleeping men with his body. It startled him when he saw the black hands of the clock closing on six-thirty. It was long since he'd slept so well. Gathering soap, towel, a kettle, and a fat lamp, he took the lantern and went to the stream.

When he had water in the kettle over the lamp, he threw the towel over his bare shoulders because it was cool in the cavern. He chuckled, thinking a cup of hot coffee would taste good, and wondered where the marshal's men were blistering their shoulders this day.

He went back for his shirt, another lamp and pot, and put coffee on to boil. The heat from the three lamps warmed him and he hunkered, shirt over his shoulders, and put a cigarette together.

He'd had a good night's rest but his hip was tender from the stone floor. He wondered whether Boots could spare enough hay for bedding. He was in better spirits than when he'd rolled in the night before although his anguish at his fellow man persisted. The mob had been a reversion to the time man had run in packs. Each undoubtedly thought himself a splendid fellow, a kind husband, and a thoughtful father. He couldn't fault the individuals for what the mob did. He and the band were the outcasts, and the law-abiding had a duty to protect their families. He did condemn them for their mass hysteria. Man alone was good. Collectively, he was brutal and dishonest. The only honest man was the criminal who admitted what he was.

He lit the cigarette and thought about Boots and the Preacher. The Fiddler admired Boots. The Preacher had never mentioned his past nor his family. None of them had. It must have cost the Preacher a goodly slice of pride to admit to Boots that he was a wanted man and needed refuge for himself and his companions. The Fiddler had the feeling that, with her, she'd always be loyal no matter what her kin or man had done.

Strange, that someone should murder Eli, and that the Preacher should know about the cave. Strange, too, the cave itself. What was its secret?

The Fiddler finished his cigarette, shredded it, and let the stream carry off the waste. It was a fast, full little stream, about two feet wide and about that deep. Curious, he took the lantern back to the wall where the stream spouted and found it free running from some spring deeper within the hill. The light showed a darkness near the floor a few yards from the stream and he went to examine it.

There was an aperture, less than two feet high and three feet wide. He got down on his belly and shoved the lantern inside. It was a tunnel with a downward-slanting floor. He snaked in a few feet, finding the passage tight but maneuverable. He worked his way up to his boot toes, seeing ahead a slab of stone at the bottom of the decline that seemed to bar the way although there was an opening beneath it.

The water in the kettle was warm when he returned to the lamps. He washed from it, rinsing himself with the icy stream water and toweling vigorously. It had been a week since he'd shaved, and he was beginning to feel he must look like Mac's brother. He took the lantern back to the table to search for the razor and mirror the Preacher had brought. When he didn't find them at once, he glanced to see whether the light was disturbing his partners.

The Kid was missing. His saddle, clothes, and gunbelt were gone. The Fiddler swore softly and steadily while he thrust into his shirt, buckled on his gunbelt, and clapped on his hat. The Kid had swilled too much whiskey and decided to break out on his own. He was a threat to all of them. He'd never make it by himself and when cornered was likely to make a deal for his life: His freedom in exchange for the rest of them.

The Fiddler ran down the tunnel without alerting the others. There'd be confusion and questions and he didn't have the answers. He wanted to talk with Boots, find out what she knew, when the Kid had left if she'd heard him, what horse he'd taken.

The Kid had left the wall section up. The panel was propped open with a saddle. The Fiddler recalled the boast the Kid had made about putting his brand on Boots, and a shaking heaviness filled his chest. He scrambled into the stall and ran to the barn doors. He saw the Kid on the porch with Boots and blew a gusty breath of relief. She was in the rocking chair and he was on the step. They were drinking coffee. The Kid was displaying his teeth, gesturing widely, probably boasting of his escapades, and Boots was laughing.

A slow, hot anger began to burn in the Fiddler. This time the Kid had gone too far. The Fiddler looked swiftly down the slope and scanned the road. There were no dust plumes. He walked slowly from the barn to the porch breathing deeply to calm the fury that filled him. He did not want to display his rage to Boots.

The Kid put a sly look in his eyes and a smirk on his lips when he saw the Fiddler approaching. The Fiddler ignored him.

"Morning, Boots," the Fiddler said, touching his hat. "I didn't hear your signal when you rapped."

"Of course not," she said and laughed. She was wearing a man's shirt and Levi's again and the imps were dancing in her eyes. "I haven't rapped. I thought I'd give the day a chance to happen."

He swung on the Kid and made no effort to mask his wrath. "I want a word with you inside," he ordered.

"Sure, friend," the Kid said jauntily, "when I finish my coffee."

"Now!"

The sharpness of the command startled the Kid. His eyes widened briefly and then he drew a curtain over them. "With your permission?" he murmured to Boots. He left the coffee unfinished but strolled defiantly toward the barn. The Fiddler turned to Boots and said soberly, "In an hour or two, if you see it's safe—"

"Yes," she said, leaving the rocker and coming to him.

Her lips looked red and sweet as wild strawberries. "It's time I got to my chores."

"Let them go," he suggested. "We'll help when a proper watch is posted. It will give us something to do."

"Thank you, Frank," she said and added with a little laugh, "Don't be too harsh with the boy. He meant no harm and I enjoyed talking with him. He's very amusing."

"Yes, I'm sure he is," the Fiddler said coolly and walked to the barn. He fought his temper, determined not to erupt. The Kid was waiting for him just inside the doors.

"Hey friend," the Kid said, half protesting, half wheedling. "You are hopping mad. What have I done?"

The Fiddler had himself in hand. "You endangered all of us including Boots," he said with a calm he did not feel.

"I did not think—" the Kid began and flashed a smile. "But of course, that is it. I did not think."

"That is it," the Fiddler said dryly. "Let's not expose ourselves any longer."

"Of course, friend," the Kid said quickly. He ran ahead to the stall and scurried under it. The saddle was pulled away and the section thudded down.

The Fiddler had the panel up again when Boots said at his back, "I'll scratch the hay around." She laid her hand lightly on his arm. "Don't let your anger confuse your reason."

He nodded curtly without speaking and started into the tunnel.

"Frank?"

He turned his head over his shoulder.

"When you shave leave the mustache." She was laughing.

He was furious with Boots, with the Kid, with himself when he stepped into the cave. He'd have been shaved and presentable if the Kid hadn't run out.

The Kid had thrown his saddle against the wall and was sitting against it, looking at his boot toes and smoking a cigarette. The Preacher, Jake, and Mac were standing in their socks, pulling their pants over their shirttails. They were staring at the Kid. Their eyes were opaque and their lips were thin.

The Preacher sat on a cartridge case to work into his twelve-inch black boots. His face was stony and lines were graven in it. He asked coldly, "What happened, Frank?"

"You tell it, Kid," the Fiddler said.

The Kid ground his cigarette out on the floor and put on a shame-faced look but challenge lurked in his eyes. "I made a mistake. I went out by myself for some air."

"Why'd you take your saddle?" Jake asked fiercely.

"Why, to prop up the feedbox so I could scoot back in if anybody was around," the Kid said. He sounded surprised at the question.

"You went outside without the signal from Boots," the Preacher said severely. "There was no lookout. You didn't know there wasn't someone nosing around. If someone had been there and taken you, they'd have found the tunnel, and the rest of us wouldn't have had a chance. You put Boots in danger as well as the rest of us. We made some rules last night. You broke all of them."

"He's lower'n a sheep dipper," Mac growled.

"Right now we ain't a outlaw band," Jake said. "We're a army and we're at war. In the Army they shoot a man that doesn't follow orders."

"Or string him up," Mac said. "He's due to be strung up anyhow."

The Fiddler smelled coffee and went to the streamside for the pot. He filled five cups and took one to the Kid. To the others he said, "Pull up a bench. Sitting calms a man.

Drinking coffee gives him something to do with his hands."
He sat beside the Preacher.

The Kid took a swallow of coffee, looked at his toes, and
finally looked toward the table. His forehead was wrinkled
and he looked abashed. He said meekly, "I did wrong but
nobody was hurt and I learned my lesson. I'll follow the
rules, I promise." A thought crossed his mind and he
showed a quick smile, winking an eye. "It was the widow.
She led me on. There's a lively mare that's broke to double
harness and no stud in her pasture. She made me lose my
mind."

The Fiddler fought back the bile that fermented in his
stomach. The Preacher blanched under his weather stain.
Jake and Mac went rigid.

The Preacher recovered first. He said icily, "We are here
under the sufferance of Mrs. Carrington. You will in no
way jeopardize our position. In the future you will not
speak to her unless she addresses you." Uncharacteris-
tically, he added, "She is off your range, cowboy. Get that
through your head."

"Hey, why the ruckus?" the Kid asked in a hurt voice.
And when chill silence met his words, he said quickly,
"Sure, friend. I got it all. Count on me."

The Fiddler could find no sincerity in anything the Kid
had said. The Fiddler distrusted him more than before.
The Kid would be resentful and vengeful. Because they
still had to live together, he said moderately, "Kid, you've
had a look at the lay of the land in daylight. What would
be the best place for a lookout?"

The Kid looked downcast but after a moment said,
"The tree. Up there in the branches of that ponderosa."

The Fiddler laughed without humor. "I agree, except
the trunk is too thick and it's a long way up. I couldn't

climb it." He looked at the Preacher, who lifted his withered arm, and at Mac, who hugged his bear fat, and at Jake, who considered the two fingers of his left hand.

"I can make it," the Kid said. He sounded eager. "Barefooted, I can climb like a monkey."

It was a gamble. The Fiddler had no faith in the Kid's reliability but it seemed the only way to make him feel a member of the band again. "All right, Kid," he said quietly. "It's your responsibility."

"Friend, I have the eyes of the eagle," the Kid boasted, some of his bravado returning. "Have no fear. The Kid will watch over you."

The Fiddler soaked the blanket for the sliding panel, and the Preacher fried bacon, then heated biscuits and finally scrambled two dozen eggs. They were finishing coffee with cigarettes when three raps sounded on the feedbox. The Kid jumped off his cartridge case.

"I'll answer the door," the Fiddler said wryly. If there was resentment in the Kid's eyes it was veiled.

When Boots reported only normal traffic on the road, he crawled into the stall and stood beside her. She had changed to a full-skirted pale green and pink gingham dress and wore a matching sunbonnet. She looked very feminine.

"Did you smell bacon and coffee?" he asked.

"Not a trace," she assured him. "You're comfortable and eating well?"

He laughed. "Mind if we pitch some hay down from the loft? The bedsprings are stiff."

"By all means," she said. "Is there anything you need?"

"You're going to town," he assumed.

"Yes, since you volunteered to do the chores." Her eyes twinkled with amusement. "I'd planned to weed the garden today. It'll be like an oven out there."

"Do us good to work some of the chill out of our bones," he said. "Don't do anything out of the ordinary."

"I'm taking in some vegetables. I always do on Fridays."

"Don't go anywhere you wouldn't normally. Don't ask questions."

"Yes, *sir!*" she said saucily and saluted. "I'll report when I return from the enemy camp."

He laughed ruefully. "I had that coming. Giving orders isn't my way. Nor obeying them. We'll get the team and help you load."

"How did I ever manage before without my crew?" she asked, lifting her hands helplessly. "The team is hitched and the wagon loaded."

"Be careful," he said. He lifted the feedbox and hesitated before crawling into the tunnel. "Boots?"

"Yes?"

"I'd like to talk with you sometime. About Eli."

Distant memory briefly troubled her eyes but the shadows were gone as quickly as they had come. "Of course," she said. "When I come back."

He dropped to his knees and she started out. From the middle of the barn she turned and called, "Don't forget what I told you about your mustache."

He heard her laughing as she went out the door. Damnit, he'd meant to shave after breakfast.

The wagon was rattling down the two ruts that cut into the long rocky slope to the road when the Fiddler returned to the barn with the band. He thought the Kid had darted a suspicious look at him when he'd reported his conversation with Boots but he'd made no comment. Now, after searching the road, the Kid ran to the ponderosa, shucked his hat, boots, and socks and shinnied up the trunk, bracing the soles of his feet against it and hoisting himself with his arms. He went up quickly and disappeared in the high branches. Jake pitched down hay, and Mac and the Fiddler carried it to the blankets.

"The Kid reports all clear," the Preacher said when the three of them joined him at the doors. "I hope you haven't given him more load than he can carry, Frank." He had a dog with him. "She's Heidi," he added, nodding in the dog's direction.

"I wouldn't turn my back to that Kid," Jake said, twisting the ends of his mustache.

"We should of shot him," the usually amiable Mac grunted.

"It's his hide as well as ours," the Fiddler said without conviction. "I don't think they can see us from the road but it's best if we keep behind the house."

The Preacher had found two hoes and a spade. He led Jake and Mac to the garden. The Fiddler climbed the hill behind the barn and stretched out to study the surroundings. The sun flamed with a white intensity that burned the color from the sky, and the thought passed through the Fiddler's head that nothing could be better on such a day than a cold glass of beer in the comfort of the cavern. He surveyed the land to the west first. Barren, open, scorched hills rolled in mounting waves to the horizon. It would be impossible to approach undetected from that direction. To the north, the bench ran for perhaps a mile before it merged into the hillside. There were no trees nor cover. What grass there was had burned crisp except along the stream that gushed from the hillside and flowed through the middle of the land. Beside the water, the grass was green and lush and here half a dozen cows and several calves munched with the three horses. It was a sorry ranch.

The only blind spot the Fiddler could detect was the dry

gulley to the south, which they'd crossed the night before after breaking out of the stand of pine. He could not see down the embankment and into it and he remembered that the buildings on the bench had not been visible until they reached the top. He bellied down the hill and hallooed the Kid from the foot of the ponderosa.

"Nothing coming," the Kid called down from among the three-needle bunched boughs. "I got my eyes peeled."

"Can you see the trail to the south? The way we came last night."

"Oh sure," the Kid sang cockily. "I can make it out easy. Into the gulley and all the way to the pines."

"If they come that way," the Fiddler said, "it means they're suspicious. There's nothing on that trail but this place. If there's anything on that trail that doesn't look right, don't wait until you're sure. Sing out and come down fast. Don't forget to pick up your hat and shoes."

"Fiddler," the Kid called, out of reach high in the tree, "you're worse than a mother hen."

The Preacher was working in the garden right along with Jake and Mac, chopping weeds between the rows of stunted corn. He held the hoe in his strong right hand and steadied the handle with his crippled arm. All three of them were breathing in short dry gasps and sweat ran down their cheeks. Jake had removed his hat, and his white skull was covered with oily beads. The ends of his great mustache drooped. Mac grunted every time he turned a spade of dirt.

The Fiddler had intended relieving the Preacher but withheld the offer. The Preacher would have interpreted it as deference to his arm. "I'll spell you, Jake," he said instead. "Take time to build a smoke. When you've cooled off, give Mac a breather. He can take over from the

Preacher." When Jake handed him the hoe, the Fiddler added quietly, "Go up on the hill behind the barn. Keep your eyes open, especially south on the trail we used."

Jake's black eyebrows lifted. He looked toward the high branches of the ponderosa and bobbed his head decisively before he covered it with his hat and ambled toward the hill.

The morning sizzled. The sun was past noon high, and the Fiddler was about to call a dinner halt in the coolness of the cavern when the Kid called, "Dust trail on the road. The widow's wagon, I guess."

"We don't take chances," the Fiddler called back at once. "Come on down. Rest of you, pick up whatever you've dropped and let's make tracks."

"It's the widow," the Kid shouted. "I'll stay. Nobody'll look for me up here anyway."

"They would when they saw your hat and boots," the Fiddler said angrily. "Slide down."

"Hey friend," the Kid said. "Favor me. Take them inside."

The Preacher strode to the foot of the tree. He was uncommonly taut. His voice was quiet but razor-edged. "Get down, Kid," he said, "or I'll shoot you down."

From the hilltop where he'd been lying, Mac roared, "Turned off the road and coming this way fast. It's got to be the posse."

VI

There was nothing they could do but wait. No one felt like eating and they were sitting tense and silent around the table when three sharp raps sounded on the panel.

"I told you it was the widow," the Kid muttered sullenly, starting for the tunnel. The Fiddler caught him by the belt, cuffed him, and sent him sprawling.

Hatred flared in the Kid's eyes when he sat up but he quickly put on a look of injured innocence. He said softly, "I don't know why you did that."

"Stay put until you're told what to do," the Fiddler said sharply. He wheeled and hurried through the tunnel.

When the Fiddler lifted the sliding panel and poked his head under it, he was nose to nose with Boots. She was squatting in the stall, peering into the opening. Her eyes teased mischievously. He crawled out smiling and they stood facing one another.

"A greeting like that when a man opens his eyes in the morning could make his whole day right," he said.

"Frank!" she exclaimed and looked demurely at her toes but before she lowered her head he saw the beginning of an impish smile playing at the corners of her lips.

He laughed without restraint, a buoyant, happy laugh that felt good. His normal, carefree exuberance came surging back. Boots was outrageous and she delighted him. He wrapped his hands around her trim waist, lifted her, and whirled her around the stall, full skirt billowing. She was laughing when he put her on her feet but her eyes turned solemn and her hand lingered on his arm before she stepped back.

"I wasn't followed and there's only the usual traffic on the road," she said, quite serious now.

"Why were you running the team?" he asked. "From the dust, we thought it was the posse."

"They'll be coming," she said. "I was in a hurry to warn you. The town is in an uproar."

"I expected it," the Fiddler said.

"They're afraid of a shootout because they know you're armed." She glanced at his gunbelt. "Every man in town is wearing a gun, even the shopkeepers. There are no women or children on the street. It's a very nervous town."

"I can't say I'm sorry," he said. "They thought it was going to be a carnival."

"They found the ponies in the marshal's stable." She smiled. "He was furious. No other horses have been reported stolen so he's convinced you're on foot. The posse is ransacking the town. Then they'll start searching the hills and ranches. We're close. I think we can expect a call this afternoon or tomorrow morning."

"Or tonight," he said soberly. "You up to it?"

"I can face them down." There was no playfulness in her now. Her eyes were determined. "The marshal is wild-eyed. He's acting like a madman. The townspeople are just as frenzied. They'd make you suffer terribly if they caught you. I know you're outlaws but I don't think you're as bad as they say. I know my uncle and he isn't bad. He admires you and I trust his judgment. I don't want to see you hurt, Frank."

Had she felt it too, that strange harmony at the moment

of their meeting? He tried to read her eyes but there was nothing in them except a normal concern. "I think we'd better stay inside until they've searched here thoroughly," he said. "When they've been here, give them plenty of time to move on before you signal. If they seem at all suspicious, wait a day if necessary. Now go take another look. If the way is clear, I'll give you a hand with the team."

She laughed. "Already done. Unhitched and turned to pasture. I'll just go about my usual chores. The garden looks better than it has all year."

"Then I'd better get back," he said. "The others will be wondering."

"I'll pitch the hay around again." She looked thoughtful. "I'll put a cow and calf in the stall. There's one calf that's sickly. It would do better out of the hot sun."

"You please me," he said and chuckled. "A man doesn't stand a chance against you."

A quick smile started to acknowledge his remark and as quickly vanished. She said quite solemnly, "If they're here this afternoon, you can come to the porch tonight." She turned so he could not see her eyes. "For the talk you wanted."

A very wet blanket slapped his face when he crawled under the feedbox. The Kid was standing just beyond.

"What the hell you doing here?" the Fiddler demanded angrily, coming out of the crawl space and standing to face him.

"Hey friend," the Kid said. There was a sarcastic tone in the lilt of his voice. "The blanket, you know? It needed more water to take up the smell of the cooking."

The Fiddler's frayed nerves snapped. "You damned sneak," he fumed. "You came here to listen."

"I heard the hanky-panky with the widow." The Kid's

voice hissed between his teeth. "Stay away from her or I'll put a blade between your ribs." He swung about and ran ahead before the Fiddler could slap him down.

When the Kid entered the cave, the Fiddler heard him whistling a bar from "Yavapai Pete." By the time the Fiddler reached the cavern, the Kid was doing a crazy-step jig toward the table and singing a few lines:

Well, Pete fanned his gun fast but they got him at last,
And he died with his boots on his feet.
The Wild West was rid of a dangerous kid
With the shootin' of Yavapai Pete.

At the table, Mac laughed heartily and Jake allowed himself to smile. Even the Preacher looked relaxed.

"What did Boots find out?" the Preacher asked.

He told them they could expect a visit and explained they'd have to remain inside for a time.

The Kid took the coffee pot and started for the stream. To the Fiddler he said, "Break out the fiddle and scrape up a tune. Long as we're in this hole, let's be happy rats."

"Bring back the stew pot," the Preacher told the Kid. To the Fiddler he said, "Think you could play a tune, Frank? It would help pass the time."

The Fiddler frowned and shook his head. "I'd like to," he said, certain the Kid had known he'd have to decline. "That blanket may keep the cooking smells out of the barn but I'm afraid the resonance from the strings might get through."

"Oh sure, that's right," the Kid dismissed his suggestion. He clicked his heels and did some fancy footwork on his way back to the table with the stew kettle. "Got to give you credit, Fiddler. You think of everything."

They were sopping up the gravy from their plates when the Fiddler asked the Preacher, "Where's that other tunnel go?"

"Didn't know there was one," the Preacher said.

The Fiddler walked him over and showed him the small entrance. The Preacher squatted and pushed a lantern into the opening as the Fiddler had done. "Another small cave, I'd suppose," he said, getting back up. He seemed to be measuring the Fiddler's shoulders, a half smile playing at his lips. "Don't get any ideas, Frank," he warned. "I'm pint-sized and I wouldn't crawl in there. Know anything about spelunking?"

"Maybe," the Fiddler said, "if you'll tell me what it means."

"Exploring caves," the Preacher said seriously. "Some people do it as a pastime. Even with experienced spelunkers, it can be dangerous. Men have been known to go into a hole in the ground and never come out again. There were caves along the Mississippi back in Illinois. When we were boys, we didn't play cowboys and Indians. We played pirates and buried treasure. There was this one big cave, a broad opening from a ledge above the river. We found some tunnels off it, one a very small tunnel like this one. We were all sizes. One of the smallest—his name was Bruce—had read a book about a king named Bruce who'd hidden in a cave, and nothing would do until he'd crawled through that tunnel to see if he could discover a cave for his very own. He took a candle and went in. The tunnel was about twenty feet long. The farther he crawled, the narrower the tunnel became. He squeezed through the last few feet and popped out like a cork from a bottle.

"He was in a small cave of no special interest and when he'd had his look, he found he couldn't get back into the tunnel. He tried backing out feet first but no matter how he scraped and twisted, his shoulders wouldn't fit. We could hear him hollering and crying and we got panicky. We wouldn't admit it to each other but we were afraid to tell our folks what had happened. We'd been forbidden to crawl into tunnels. We figured what we'd do was to rig up a long pole with a board on the end and push through food and water and blankets to Bruce for the rest of his life. Luckily for Bruce, one of the older boys had a grain of sense and told his father what had happened. It took six men working in shifts around the clock two days to chisel that tunnel large enough to get Bruce out because, of course, they had to make it big enough to fit them while they worked. They pushed through food and water like we'd planned and they kept shouting encouragement to him. It was only forty-eight hours Bruce was entombed but he was paper-white and couldn't stop shaking and staring wild-eyed when they pulled him out. He never was quite right after that."

"Poor boy," the Fiddler said sympathetically and then he laughed. "It's good to know that if I do go in there and get stuck, all I'd have to do is wait until you fellows dig me out. It'd give you something to do."

"I wouldn't bank on it, Frank," the Preacher said severely. "There are veins of quartz and granite in these hills. If that tunnel is a pocket in that kind of rock, we'd have to blast."

"I think you have restrained my curiosity about tunnels," the Fiddler told the Preacher. In the back of his mind he wondered why there had been such specific and detailed warning.

The Kid came to the stream with their dinner dishes and

washed them. When he'd returned to the table, the Preacher said, "He's trying."

"I guess he is," the Fiddler conceded but added, "It's hard to forget the remarks he made about Boots."

"I know," the Preacher said. "I haven't told him she's my niece."

"That, Milford, is not the point," the Fiddler said. "He should not have said those things about any woman."

The Preacher sighed. "Of course you're right. I think he regrets the way he'd talked and acted."

Jake and Mac had rolled up and the Fiddler went to his blankets and saddle. He quickly fell asleep. When he awakened there was a commotion that rolled down the tunnel from the barn, and a stillness in the cave. Jake and Mac were on their heels, and their guns were drawn. The Kid's face was pallid.

"I think they've found the entrance," the Preacher said.

"Relax," the Fiddler said quickly. He hadn't told them about the cow and calf Boots was going to put in the stall. "I'll check."

He hurried down the tunnel, pulled aside the blanket, and listened. He heard the sound of shifting weight, boards being pushed, shuffling hooves, and then three raps. He lifted the panel, put his head under it, and looked at Boots hunkered between two sets of four legs.

"I hoped it might be you," she said. She was back in shirt and Levi's.

"This is getting cozy," he said as the calf lowered its head and slopped his face.

"It's working," she said. She looked pleased with herself. "If anyone should be watching, it gives me an excuse to be in and out of the barn. No visitors yet but there's a good-sized dust cloud hanging in the air toward town. If it's the posse, I'll let you know when they're gone."

"Give them ample time." He repeated the caution he'd sounded earlier.

"See you tonight," she promised and smiled.

He lowered the panel. The cow and calf shifted and the cow lowed. The others were still tense when he returned and he laughed to put them at their ease. He told them about the puny calf and cow now occupying the stall.

"That is rare," the Kid exclaimed and laughed boisterously. "A widow, a cow, and a sick calf to protect us!"

After a moment, the Fiddler said, "We'd better hold it down. The posse is on its way."

The Kid's eyes slitted and his lips pressed thin. He shrugged and said, "What about some poker and whiskey to pass the afternoon?"

"That sounds like you held all the hands last night," the Fiddler said.

Jake twisted the ends of his mustache. "I'm out thirty dollars," he grumbled. "Mac dropped ten and the Preacher five. I'd like a chance to get even."

"It's a trap but I'll play," Mac said.

The Preacher nodded his head and reached for the cards and the chips.

"You sitting in today, friend?" the Kid asked the Fiddler.

"I'll take a hand later," the Fiddler said. "There are some things like shaving I didn't get done this morning."

The Kid's eyes darted darkly toward him but he made no comment. The Kid undoubtedly had heard Boots' invitation to come to the porch. The Fiddler took a lantern, fat lamp, kettle, mirror, soap, and razor to the stream and sat against the stone wall to smoke a cigarette while the water heated. Despite the Preacher's pointed warning, the small tunnel lured him. If it led to another chamber, there was no guessing what it might hold. Ancient stone spearheads, implements, perhaps a burial place with fragments of sacred cloth clinging to crumbling bones. When he'd shaved, defiantly leaving the mustache hairs on his upper lip, and washed his shirt in the same hot water, he spread it on the floor beside the fat lamp and took the lantern to the tunnel. The others were bent over their cards, and the Preacher did not call caution. The Fiddler pulled off his boots and gunbelt and, bare-chested, wriggled into the opening, pushing the lantern ahead.

For the first eight or ten feet, the floor of the narrow tunnel dropped sharply. He felt the walls and the ceiling pressing his shoulders. Abruptly, the passageway appeared to be blocked by a slab of gray stone. When he reached it, he found the tunnel continued under it. He clawed his way to the stone. It looked like granite. He measured the dimensions of the passage and judged it to be about one foot high and a little more than two feet wide—merely a slit in the bowels of the earth. He shook his head and started to back out but something strangely drew him onward. He extended the lantern to the full length of his arm into the fissure. Beyond the thrust of granite the light reflected on walls and floor of creamy white stone. It looked to be a hewn corridor. Without hesitation, he dragged himself under the few feet of granite and walked upright in the dazzling splendor of gleaming quartz. His breath was coming in short, shallow spurts when he stepped from the passage into a small round chamber and held the lantern aloft.

Like the corridor, the cave had been hacked from quartz, which gleamed except for a dark streak at the far side above a spring that gushed from the stone. He lowered the

lantern and inspected the floor. Although awed by the
beauty, he felt vaguely disappointed. The room appeared
to be clean-swept. He crossed the room, holding the lantern high and thinking the ancient ones had traced the
course of the stream and found its source. He held the lantern toward the dark and gleaming streak above the spout-
ing spring and gasped. It was a mother lode of pure gold.

The vein had been worked in recent years, he saw, lean-
ing closer to examine the markings of a sharp tool in the
soft metal. Pure gold had been taken from the lode. His
toe touched something heavy yet yielding on the floor and
he lowered the lantern. A sizable leather pouch lay on the
floor and near it, a mallet and a chisel. He hefted the
buckskin bag. It was weighty. When he loosened the
drawstrings he found as he'd expected that it was filled
with gold shavings. Eli had discovered the secret of the ancient ones.

In some unguarded moment, Eli must have been indis-
creet. Someone had suspected Eli had a fortune on the
farm but he'd never found it.

The Fiddler sat on the floor with the bag of gold cradled
between his legs, its weight at once a burden on his mind
and heart. Boots was a very wealthy woman. He did not
want her to be rich. It made a vast difference in any rela-
tionship they ever could enjoy. It made a difference, too, in
his association with the others in the band. He could not
reveal his discovery to any of them, not even to the
Preacher. A man would kill his brother for far less. The
Fiddler did not know what to do. He wished miserably and
vainly that he'd never crawled through the tunnel into this
treasure trove.

He thought he heard his name called, distant and
muffled, and he started in fear. He tied the pouch again

and left it behind, running with the lantern from the quartz cave and through the corridor. As he neared the small passage that ran under the granite monolith, he recognized the Preacher's voice.

"Frank, are you all right?" It sounded as if the Preacher's head were within the tunnel.

The Fiddler slid feet first under the pressing slab of granite, pulling the lantern after him and deliberately punishing his back and shoulders against the walls and roof and grating his chest on the floor. When he was free of the stone and backing up toward the aperture, he called, "Coming. It's all right now."

The Preacher had warned him, gone to great lengths to caution him not to enter this tunnel. He wondered whether the Preacher knew about the lode of gold and had killed his niece's husband for it. It was a shocking, unbidden thought and it saddened him to know that doubt of all mankind had cast its eternal shadow on his mind.

"What happened, Frank?" the Preacher asked when the Fiddler pushed back into the cavern, panting and bleeding. The Preacher sounded honestly concerned. "I couldn't see you or the lantern. Did you find another cave?" He noticed the Fiddler's wounds and blew out his breath. "You got stuck. You're cut to shreds. I'll heat some water. Scrub off the lacerations. Whiskey will do for an antiseptic."

The Fiddler had left his makings with his gunbelt and boots and had a smoke going when the Preacher came back with the whiskey jug. "I can use a belt of that before you waste it on my bruises," he said and gulped a satisfying swallow. The Preacher waited anxiously for him to speak. He had another drink and filled his lungs with smoke. "You couldn't see the light or me because I plugged the hole." He grinned ruefully, knowing the deception was only the beginning of the ruses he'd have to use. "The tunnel slants down to a chunk of granite. I thought I could squeeze under."

"Could you?" the Preacher asked—too quickly, it seemed.

"Couldn't make it," the Fiddler answered and shrugged. "For a while, I thought I was in my grave."

"You damned fool!" The Preacher sounded angry. "Look at you." He'd brought a towel and soaked it with whiskey. When he cleansed the bleeding cuts, they stung and ached with the treatment. "If you'd gone another foot, we'd never have been able to free you." He paused, put the jug back in the Fiddler's hand, and said gruffly, "Don't try that again, Frank."

"I won't," the Fiddler said. "I'm still suffering." Abruptly, he noticed the stillness in the chamber and he glanced toward the table. He saw no one there nor rolled up in his blanket. "Where are the others?" he demanded, pulling on his boots and reaching for his gunbelt.

"At the feedbox," the Preacher said. "The posse is here digging through the barn."

VII

When the Fiddler had dropped the feedbox behind him,
Boots had leaned against a post and drawn a fluttery
breath. She hoped he hadn't noticed, but she was badly
frightened. Her legs did not feel substantial enough to bear
her weight. It had reminded her that her dog, Heidi, had
taken such a friendly interest in her uncle that she'd followed him about the place constantly when he was there
before the jailbreak. She'd found the dog sniffing at the
bottom of the feedbox panel when she'd returned from
town, and she'd had to tie her at the ponderosa.

After an insecure moment, Boots hurried to the house,
changed into shirt and Levi's, and waded through the
waves of heat that quivered from the baked earth toward
the pasture. Heidi, panting and miserable, begged to go
along. It tore at Boots' heart but she refused to take the
risk. She led the cow and calf to the barn, raked the hay in
the stall, and filled the bin. After she'd placed a pail of
water between the cattle, she started toward the doors. The
two hoes and spade the men had used were leaned against
the wall. Newly bruised weeds were imbedded in dry lumps
of dirt on all the blades. Nervous apprehension clutched
her heart. How many other telltale signs had been left
behind? She scoured the spade and one hoe with hay until
the steel was bright and clean and took the second hoe to
the garden. The long rows of fresh-turned dirt in the newly

weeded garden dismayed her. It had not been a lone woman but four stalwart men who'd worked in the garden that morning.

It was midafternoon, the hottest time of another sun-seared day, a time when even the cows had sense enough to crowd close to the cool stream and lie down. She had hoed furiously, reworking along a row of corn, merely turning the dirt so it would be apparent that furrow had not been done at the same time as the others, when she heard the sound of hoofbeats on the slope. She dropped the hoe at the end of the row and ran toward the house. Heidi lifted her head, tongue dripping, eyes pleading, and whined piteously. Boots left her at the tree and slumped on the floor of the porch in scant shade. Her face was flushed, her shirt and pants drenched with perspiration when the posse clomped into the yard in choking swirls of dust.

The riders had come up from the stage road in the blinding glare of the sun, and Marshal Fargo, astride a heaving buckskin, squinted around the yard and at the house. His stony face was caked with dust, and streams of sweat made tracks down his cheeks. There were ten riders in the party, all looking grim and weary and breathing almost as hard as the horses. Knowing the marshal didn't see her, Boots pushed to her feet and started toward him.

"Widow Carrington," he said gruffly, touching the brim of his hat as she neared.

"Step down," she said, struggling to be cordial, "you and your men. I'll get a bucket of cool water and a dipper. There's the trough at the pump if you want to water the horses."

"Thank you kindly," he said and climbed down, waving his men from their saddles. "You don't appear surprised to see a marshal's posse ride into your yard."

"I was expecting you. I was in town this morning and heard the talk," she said, starting toward the porch.

"Have you seen anything?" Fargo asked intently. "Have they been by here?"

"Not a soul," she said. He plodded with her to the house and she brought the water pail and dipper from the kitchen.

The riders trailed their ponies to the trough and when they'd drunk, spread themselves along the edge of the porch. They seemed disheartened and dispirited, as if the heat had burned all the zeal from them.

When the marshal had his dipper, she took him to the end of the porch, motioned him to the rocker, and sat on the floor with her back to the wall. "A terrible thing, this trouble," she murmured.

"Yes," he said. The sun blindness seemed to have left his eyes and he examined her sternly. She was breathing heavily from her exertion and didn't have to act. "You look done in," he observed.

"I am," she admitted. "I've been weeding the garden."

"In this awful heat!" The lines about his set mouth were deep and downturned.

"I have to," she said. "No worse for me than you. You've been riding hard in the sun."

"We can't rest until we recapture those murderers," he said fiercely. "They're desperate men and they're armed. No one's safe, especially a widow, alone, like you. We'll not overlook an inch of this place. For all you know, they may have slipped in while you were in town."

"I'd be obliged," she said quietly, "although I'm certain they're not here. As you see, the land's all open. That only leaves the house and barn."

The men had taken out the makings and built smokes.

The marshal called to four of them, "Jim, Ed, Ben, Al, you go through the barn. If there's hay in the loft, you know what to do." To a fifth, he said, "Beau, come into the house with me. Rest of you, spread out and be ready with your guns, in case we turn them up and they come out shooting."

The riders climbed to their feet slowly and the marshal went into the house with the pock-faced kid called Beau. They were back on the porch in a few minutes. The marshal shook his head at Boots and started toward the barn. She walked with him.

"You'd best stay under cover, inside the house," he growled.

"There's no one," she said. "Even if the outlaws were here, they wouldn't shoot a woman."

"These would," the marshal said. His eyes narrowed. "In all my years as a lawman, I never saw a meaner pack. Come along but stay behind us."

When they neared the garden, Boots braced herself for the questions the marshal was sure to ask. He glanced idly at the plot, paused to study it, and then confronted her grim-faced. "You didn't do all that yourself," he sharply accused. "Thought you said you were in town. Who helped you?"

"I can't afford a hired hand," she flared. "Of course I did it by myself. Who would there be to help me? I was working those rows at sunup. Finished the corn this afternoon."

He turned to consider the garden some more and then his eyes found Heidi at the ponderosa. The dog's jaws were open and her tongue was in the dirt. "Widow Carrington," he swung and said angrily, "I cannot abide any person who disfavors animals. Why have you tethered the dog out there in the heat without water?"

"I'm sorry," she said miserably. "I truly am. She was in the way. I forgot her when I almost collapsed."

When she did not move to the dog at once, he snapped, "Untie her now!" and strode on to the barn.

Boots was crying when she stroked Heidi. The dog swept dry needles with her tail, licked Boots' hand, got up, and shook herself. Boots started toward the house, meaning to give Heidi a drink from the bucket and put her inside. The dog walked at her heels for a few steps and then turned and trotted to the barn. Boots gasped and hurried after her.

In the barn, the marshal and Beau were standing in the middle of the dirt floor watching the opening to the loft, two men with pitchforks climbed down, wheezing and sneezing and sweating profusely. "Nothing up there," one reported.

Boots didn't see Heidi and knew she was in the stall. Two men stood beside it. One had a pale face and looked like a shopkeeper, although he wore a gunbelt. The other had a deep-tanned face and looked like a rancher.

The pale-faced man called out to Boots, "Why you got this cow and calf in here?"

The weathered man spat disgustedly and said scornfully, "She's took that puny calf in out of the sun with its mamma at its side."

The marshal went to the stall and looked in. "What's that dog sniffing around for?" he asked intently and turned his glacial eyes on Boots.

Boots felt the perspiration on her forehead turn cold. "That's her pail I put in there," Boots said in a voice she managed to keep firm.

"Then why isn't she drinking from it?" the marshal asked, openly hostile.

The cattleman answered for her, "Because the cows been using it."

"Heidi!" Boots commanded with all the strength she could summon. The dog hesitated, came out under the cow, and lay at Boots' feet.

"Odd," the marshal persisted, "the way that dog kept nosing around that stall."

"I told you it was her pail," Boots said, voice weakening.

"Might be a trapdoor covered by that hay," the marshal said, crafty-eyed and cold.

"You accusing me of hiding those outlaws?" Boots shrilled.

"Only thinking of your safety, Widow Carrington," the marshal said, mercilessly calm, and lifted his .44 from the holster. "Men, take the cattle out of the stall. Pitch away the hay. Look close now, men. If the trapdoor moves an inch we fill it full of lead."

Sidestepping as he moved, the storekeeper gingerly pitched all the hay from the stall. There was nothing but the packed dirt floor and straws stuck into the bottom of the feedbox. The marshal glowered, holstered his gun, and started to stomp away.

"You pitch that hay back in where it belongs," Boots shouted.

"Do what she says," the marshal ordered and left the barn. His face was gray granite when he faced the men in the yard. "Climb up," he called. He walked to his mustang and swung his leg over the saddle. To Boots, who had followed, he said with a frown, "Thank you, Widow Carrington. Hope we haven't discomforted you."

At Boots' side, Heidi snarled at him. Hoping to learn something that would be of value to the band, Boots managed to say calmly, "You did your duty, Marshal. It is a demanding task to perform."

The men straggled to their horses.

"It is a thankless task," the marshal growled but he did not seem displeased with her remark.

"How far must you go today?" she asked.

"As far as light takes us," he said resolutely. "If we don't turn them up by sundown, we'll bed where we are and press on in the morning."

"But you're traveling north," she said and wiped perspiration from her face with her forefinger. "How do you know they haven't gone south?"

"We covered that stretch last night," he said, "right after they escaped. They couldn't have gotten through us. Anyway, the deputy's down there now with another posse. We've boxed them in." He considered her briefly and his stern face softened by a faint wrinkle. "Stay out of the sun for the rest of the day. You've already done too much for a mite."

VIII

The Fiddler and the Preacher had crowded into the crawl space near the feedbox panel with the others, listening tensely. Most of the conversation was clearly audible and the Fiddler glanced at the Preacher in alarm when the marshal called attention to Heidi. They sat stiff and silent while the pitchfork picked at the hay only inches away.

When the marshal's men had shuffled out and there no longer was sound of movement in the barn except an occasional bump against the sides of the stall, the Kid squirmed around and started to speak. The Fiddler clapped his hand over the Kid's mouth and shook his head. The Kid scowled darkly and muttered under his breath. After at least five minutes had passed, they started back to the cavern, one by one.

"Why'd you slap my face?" the Kid asked when they were crossing to the table.

The Kid's continual stupidity infuriated the Fiddler. He said, "Kid, how you lived so long is a mystery. You don't show a grain of sense. Everything you do is wrong. For all we knew, one of them might have stayed behind. If you don't stop being careless, you'll get all of us killed."

The Kid glared at him. "Stop ordering me around, friend, or you're sure to wake up dead."

Mac sat on a cartridge case and sighed heavily. He ran fingers through the tangled bush of his beard and fluttered his lips. "It gets mighty close," he said. "We're burrs under each others' butts. We only been here a day and my nerves is rubbed raw already. I'm dryer'n a mud hen on a tin roof. Pour out the redeye, Preacher, and let's get back to the game."

The Preacher looked at the Fiddler, who said, "We can use a touch to ease the strain. Just so long as no one takes on a load. We've all got to stay alert."

"You worry too much, friend," the Kid told him and then examined him closely. "You look like you been wrestling with a bear. You get stuck in that little tunnel?"

"Yep," the Fiddler admitted readily. "The Preacher had to drag me out by my heels."

The Kid brayed and slapped the table. "Let's have that snort and deal the cards. You in this time, Fiddler?"

"You still winning?" the Fiddler asked.

"Sure, friend," the Kid taunted. "That scare you?"

"That it does," the Fiddler said slowly, "because I'd catch you at your winning ways and I'd have to shoot you."

"I don't cheat," the Kid screamed, overturning the cartridge case as he jumped to his feet. "Reach!"

The Fiddler's gun was in his hand. The Preacher slapped the Kid's wrist with his strong right hand, and the .44 he'd half drawn clattered to the floor. "Deal," the Preacher said.

The Fiddler took his cup of whiskey and walked to the stream. He was badly shaken. He'd wanted to squeeze the trigger and kill the Kid. No one would have faulted him if he had. He'd actually *wanted* to kill a man. He'd never felt that way before. Killing was contrary to his nature.

He made a cigarette and hunkered by a fat lamp with the coffee pot above the flame. Things he wanted to sort out were on his mind. He'd always liked the Preacher, Jake, and Mac, but now he didn't want to be with any of them.

He blamed it on the gold. He was afraid he'd say or do something that would reveal his knowledge of a tremendous discovery. One of them would associate it with his exploration of the tunnel and pry into the secret he guarded. He wanted them to hit the owlhoot trail but he didn't know how he could convince them to leave this safe hideout, even if he could round up the horses.

When he'd finished the whiskey, he poured a cup of coffee. The shirt he'd washed was dry and he put it on. He was restless and paced along the fast-running water to the far wall and back with the cup in his hand. The pouch of gold was another worry. He couldn't very well give it to Boots to be deposited in Virginia City. There'd be questions, suspicions if she didn't answer them, and a stampede if she did.

More than anything else, he decided, he wanted to quit the outlaw life, which he couldn't very well do unless he left the West forever.

It was six-thirty by the clock on the plank table when the three raps he'd been expecting sounded on the feedbox panel. Without taking his hat, he started for the corridor.

"Where you going, friend?" the Kid called from the table.

"To have a talk with Boots," the Fiddler said shortly.

"None of us leaves alone without a lookout," the Kid said and got to his feet. "You made the rule. I'll go with you."

"You'll stay where you are," the Fiddler said flatly.

"The Fiddler knows what he's doing," the Preacher said quietly. "We need to know what the posse said and did when they were here. Sit down, Kid."

The Kid was furious. "You two always got your heads together and side each other. You think you're running the gang?"

"They are," Jake said crossly. "Stop getting in the way."

Boots was waiting outside the stall when the Fiddler pushed between the cow and the calf. Heidi was with her and fluttered her tail. Boots was wearing the light gingham dress she'd had on that morning, and although the day still was hot, she looked fresh-scrubbed and cool. The elf lock was on her forehead but it was not pasted in place with perspiration.

"That was a close thing with Heidi," he said. "You thought fast on your feet."

"You heard?" Her eyes seemed to mist briefly and she bent to touch Heidi's head. "I'm afraid I've mistreated her." She straightened and said pertly, "We sent them away. I doubt they'll be back. We can sit in the shade on the porch where you can watch the road."

The late-afternoon sun was bright but the shadows from the western hills were lengthening over the brown land and there was a whisper of a breeze that ran through the Fiddler's tumbling hair.

"That was the test by fire," he said as they walked to the house. "Thank you, Boots."

"I think they left feeling sorry for me," she said and took the rocking chair. He sat on the floor against the wall and built a smoke. Abruptly, she laughed. "You shaved! And you did leave the mustache. I'm glad."

"Why?" He rubbed his upper lip. "It looks silly."

"No Frank," she said seriously. "I wasn't teasing about leaving the mustache when you shaved. With a dark mustache, hair cut short like mine and dyed black, no one in the world would recognize you."

"I hadn't thought about that," he said casually but hope

suddenly was warm in him. "Would that make a difference?"

"It would be safer." She paused and asked hesitantly, "You're not a bad man. Have you ever thought of taking another trail?"

"Maybe."

"Think of it, Frank." She wasn't pleading but she was earnest.

He sat silent and frowning. It was strange she should touch what was most on his mind.

"Is anything wrong?" she asked.

"I was thinking," he said.

"Yes?" She was waiting.

It was not the time, not here, not now, to tell her how he felt. She was too much involved as it was. He changed the subject abruptly, phrasing the question carefully. "Did Eli ever say anything about realizing a good deal of money from this place?"

At first she looked disappointed at what he said, then surprised as she reread the question, and then she laughed. "From this poor place?"

"There are possibilities," he told her. "With the spring-fed stream, you have a dependable supply of water. If you used it to irrigate the land, you could grow enough vegetables to feed the town. The cavern is cool. It would be an ideal place to store them until prices went up in the winter."

Her forehead puckered with thought. "Irrigating the land hadn't occurred to me." She paused. "Of course, I'd even forgotten about the cavern. Eli may have had something like that in mind when he made that entrance to the tunnel. He did make an odd remark one night to Eph."

"Who's Eph?" the Fiddler interrupted. He snubbed his

cigarette, shredded the butt carefully, and tossed the loose tobacco into the slight breeze.

"His brother," she said with a note of disdain in her voice. "Eli wasn't friendly with anyone and I think he even disliked and resented Eph. He'd been moderately successful as a rancher although Eli once accused him of stocking it with rustled cattle. He'd done some prospecting. One night Eph was berating Eli for his poor judgment in proving up free land so barren no one else would claim it. It upset Eli. He boasted that the day would come when he'd have more gold than Eph had ever seen. Eli may have been thinking about irrigating and storing the vegetables. I passed it off as tall talk."

It was the hint, the indiscretion the Fiddler had suspected. "How did Eph react?"

"He asked a lot of questions. I think Eli was sorry he'd made that statement. He'd say no more." She was thoughtful for a long time. "Yes, Eph must have seen the possibilities. Sometime after Eli was killed, Eph came to me with an offer to help. That should have aroused my suspicions. He doesn't like me and I don't like him and he never offered to help Eli. You see, there is a five-hundred-dollar mortgage on this place."

He broke in again. "On free land?"

"It's proved out and there are the buildings and stock." She looked troubled and irritated. "Eph paid me one hundred dollars for the option on the mortgage. If I couldn't pay it off when it fell due, he'd pay it and take the deed. I signed some papers. He knew, of course, I wouldn't be able to meet the payment."

The Fiddler was certain he knew who killed Eli. "Does Eph know about the cave?"

"No!" Boots said emphatically. "That was Eli's most closely guarded secret. No one knows."

The Fiddler disliked himself for his suspicions but he commented, "I got the impression the Preacher knew."

"Of course not," she said. "Eli didn't like Uncle Milford. He visited once, four or five years ago. They scarcely spoke to each other."

The Fiddler was relieved. The Preacher had been his friend. The Fiddler was ashamed of himself for distrusting him. He asked, "When does the mortgage fall due?"

"Soon, sometime this month, I think." She sighed. "The one hundred dollars Milford paid to use the cave will help me get away."

All the Fiddler's doubts came surging back. "But you said he didn't know about it."

"Oh. I see what you mean." She shook her head. "No. He didn't ask to use the cave. He asked if there was a place on the property, an old mine shaft, some inaccessible place where you could hide. I remembered then and showed it to him. He was very surprised and grateful."

He put the Preacher aside once more. Although he was certain Eph had killed his brother, he asked, "Do you have any suspicions about who shot Eli?"

"No. It seemed so senseless." She looked downcast and tired. "Is all this necessary?"

"I'm sorry," he said at once. "I've been thoughtless. It's been a long, difficult day for you." He stood, looking down the slope to the road where the setting sun was flinging its last rays on the gold-dust sprinkled land. "If I've seemed heartless, the things I've asked may be important. I'll go now."

"No." She smiled and her eyes brightened. "Stay and talk about other things. Tell me about yourself."

He leaned against the house and laughed. "Little enough to tell. A wandering fiddler. Going from place to place until I met the Preacher and the others and threw in with them. I thought I liked being free and footloose."

"You thought?" she prompted softly.

"Now I'm hunted and no longer free," he said pensively. "I thought it was a game but the fun is gone and I don't like the players."

He saw from the intensity of her eyes that she was concentrating but her attention had been drawn from him and she was listening to sounds he now heard: slipping rocks, the strike of iron on stone. "Frank," she whispered urgently, "someone is riding up from the gulley."

There was no time to run for the barn. The Fiddler was trapped.

IX

From outside the bedroom window at the back of the house, the Fiddler could see through the open front door. He watched a mustang paw over the embankment onto the bench. Marshal Fargo was the lone rider. The rays from the setting sun painted his face in golden red. It was a savage sculpture of burning stone. The marshal had found the trail the band had taken and tracked them to Boots' Diamond C.

Boots and Heidi walked out to meet him. Her shoulders were squared and her back was stiff.

"Evening, Widow Carrington," the marshal said solemnly. He touched his hat and stepped from the saddle.

"You came from town," Boots said in a tightly contained voice. "I thought you rode north."

"The posse did. I went back." He took off his hat as if it were a burden and pressed thumb and forefinger over closed eyes. "Mind if we sit a spell on the porch? I'm very weary."

"Of course," Boots said and the Fiddler pulled his head away before they started for the house.

The Fiddler heard the marshal's heels on the boards, and the chair rock forward when he sat on it. The Fiddler returned to the window to listen. He thought Boots must still be standing.

"It came to me when we left here," the marshal said

heavily. "Eli never rode to town by the road. With the wagon, yes, but when he rode he liked to be alone and used some back trail."

"You have doubts about me," Boots said. "That trail leads only here."

"Not you, Widow Carrington." The marshal was rocking slowly, methodically. "Eli was a good man. A poor man but honest. I have never had cause to think other of you. It occurred to me the outlaws may have used that trail for a ways before breaking west into the foothills."

"Afoot?" she said incredulously. "It isn't possible. Not into that rough, rocky country."

"How did you know they were on foot?" the marshal demanded, instantly suspicious.

"It was the talk in town," she said, cool and withdrawn.

"Yes," he recalled. "You'd been to town. We thought they were on foot. We'd have found them by now if they'd not been riding. Friends from the owlhoot must have brought horses to them."

"Did you find tracks on the trail?" Boots asked cautiously. "Had they used it at all?"

"I couldn't tell," the marshal said irritably. "It would take an ax to mark that baked clay. There were no broken twigs, no sign in the brush to show they'd gone west." He fell silent.

"Would you like coffee?" she asked more cordially. "Or a glass of cool water?"

"Thank you kindly, no," the marshal said. "I ate and had coffee in town and I must get on to the men. I only wanted to sit out of the saddle for a few moments. And to tell you not to worry about being alone. We'd have found the outlaws if they'd been anywhere near."

"You must be bone-aching tired," Boots said and the Fiddler heard her settle on the floor.

On the porch, Boots leaned back and stretched out her arms. She felt at peace for the first time that day. Her fingers were stiff from the hoeing and she flexed them and froze. The fingers of her left hand had touched the cigarette makings where Frank had left them in his hurry to hide. She could not tell whether the marshal had discovered the tobacco but he had been watching her closely. She thought she read a malicious gleam of triumph in his eyes.

"I'm tired," she said as calmly as she could against the hammering of her heart and picked up the makings. While the marshal watched with slitted eyes, she grooved the paper between thumb and forefinger, tapped in tobacco, touched the edge with her tongue, and built a smoke. She didn't stop there. She struck a lucifer. The marshal was plainly shocked. She sucked in smoke too deeply and it felt as if she'd swallowed some. It was a struggle to overcome nauseated coughing but she managed.

The marshal had watched her performance with mounting fury. Abruptly he exploded. "I'm afraid you have become quite a different person since your poor husband passed on," he said scornfully. "I am distressed to find you in such sinful ways, Widow Carrington." He strode from the porch and put the mustang to a lope.

Boots threw away the cigarette. She felt ill and didn't know whether to laugh or cry. It had been a fretful day.

Behind the house, the Fiddler had heard the marshal's outcry and was anguished. He could not imagine what Boots might have done to provoke the marshal's violent response; or what he could imagine he refused to accept.

Deep concern frayed his nerves as he waited long minutes until at last he saw the faint trail of dust on the road in the last light of the day. He ran to the porch.

"What happened, Boots?" he cried. "Tell me quickly."

She was in the rocking chair and Heidi lay beside her, tail thumping the floor. Boots' laughter was merry and her eyes were filled with devils.

"What's funny?" he asked, at once relieved and annoyed.

"The marshal's face." She caught her breath. "You heard what he said?"

"What did you do?" he insisted.

She tossed the sack of tobacco to him. "I built a smoke. You left the makings behind."

"You did what?" It was all over but he felt a chill tingle of fear in his chest. "How did you manage?"

"Eli was clumsy," she said. "I used to make them for him."

Chuckles bubbled into laughter from low in his chest. When he could manage, he said, "You, Boots, are the damndest woman I've ever known."

"Do I take that kindly?" she asked.

"You do," he said with heartfelt sincerity.

"Then I thank you, sir." Her smile was pleased. "I think we're done with the marshal. He's discouraged and the posse disheartened. I could see that in the men this afternoon. They think you've got away. He'll call off the search in another day if he doesn't tonight."

"I had the same feeling when I heard what he said." The band could ride out in safety when he'd provided the horses but there was Boots and the mortgage to consider. "Are you mortally weary, Boots?"

"A little weak after the laugh, when he'd left and it finally came," she said. "What do you want, Frank?"

"Personal attention," he said and grinned. "Oh don't look shocked. If you're up to it, I think I need a haircut."

X

"Don't shoot!"

The Fiddler put urgency in his appeal. He was standing in the tunnel at the entrance to the cavern and there was reason for his caution. Boots had accomplished a startling transformation. She'd shorn his hair, parting it in the middle and leaving bushy sideburns. With dye left over from the gingham dress she'd colored for Eli's funeral, she'd changed his hair from yellow to raven. She'd done the same for his fledgling mustache and lightly touched his eyebrows. He'd been astonished at the stranger in the mirror. He thought he looked like a riverboat gambler. She'd been pleased with her handiwork.

"The Fiddler is gone," she'd said mischievously. "I was rather fond of him. I'll feel disloyal at first but I guess I can get to know you. What's your new name?"

"Franklyn Bye," he said, still staring in the mirror and trying to get used to himself. "And it's not new. It's been my name all along."

"Good." She appraised him, smiling. "I feel more comfortable as long as you're still Frank."

Before he'd left he'd asked, "Do you have a leather pouch I could have? For my makings. Perspiration gets the tobacco damp in this weather."

She thought a moment. "Yes. Eli smoked a pipe when

he was outdoors. He had a leather tobacco pouch. I know where it is."

It was larger than he needed but he put the makings in it and thanked her.

"Good night, Franklyn Bye," she said on the porch, her hand on his arm. Her smile was sweet, not impish, and she added softly, "You've taken the first step."

Now at the entrance to the cave he called again to the others still intent on their cards, "Don't shoot."

"Don't push your luck, friend," the Kid lashed back without looking up. "Don't taunt me. Next time you won't have the Preacher to slap down my gun."

"He had the drop on you," Mac rumbled. "It was your hide the Preacher saved, not his. Only reason he didn't shoot you was, you was unarmed."

The Fiddler started toward the table. None of them yet had glanced in his direction. "I'm a changed man," he warned. "Don't go for your guns. Remember, it's me."

Curiosity aroused, the card players laid down their hands and turned their heads. The Preacher's reaction was swift and involuntary. He drew and then slowly returned the gun to the holster. "Frank, is that really you?" A pleased smile was slowly spreading the time lines on his face.

Jake stared and rubbed his hairless skull. "What'd you do with your old hair? I could make me a headpiece."

Mac ran a hand over his matted beard and tangle of hair. "Gives me a idea. Nobody knows what I look like under all this. Jake, you can have mine."

The Kid howled. "He looks like a *chihuahua*."

"More like a *caballero*," the Preacher corrected. "It's perfect, Frank. What do you have in mind?"

"The marshal was here again tonight—" the Fiddler started.

"So you went out alone, friend, and almost got us caught," the Kid shouted.

"Stop flapping your lip," Mac told him.

The Fiddler repeated what he'd overheard. "He's ready to give up the chase. In another day or two, I'm going to Carson City. Do we have enough money to buy horses, Preacher? At this point, I'd rather not steal them."

"Enough, with something left in the poke." The Preacher paused and chuckled. "Your plan worked the way you predicted, only sooner. Where do you have in mind for us to go? California?"

"Wyoming Territory," the Fiddler said promptly. He wanted the band as far away from the Diamond C as he could get them. "We have a good friend there."

"And an invitation," the Preacher remembered. "We can drift away at night, one or two at a time, and rendezvous some miles along the trail. We have ample provisions. Well. This calls for a celebration."

"I was thinking just that," the Fiddler said. "Fill up the cups. I'll sit in tonight."

"You do us a favor," the Kid said sarcastically.

"He done us all a favor, Kid," Jake said. "While we been sitting here, he's been planning. He's been too busy to play."

The Preacher was shaking the whiskey crock. "This one's almost empty." He poured a scant two fingers for each.

"Damn!" the Fiddler said.

"Oh I knew the whiskey would go and I knew this night would come," the Preacher said with a beneficent smile. "I've been hoarding a spare for such an occasion." He went to one of the provision boxes and lifted another gallon jug from behind the flour bag.

The Fiddler laughed with pleasure. "That should see us through the night."

The Preacher chuckled. "You are a changed man, Frank. All right, men, line up the cups."

That night the Kid drank heavily and lost steadily. "Don' unnerstan'," he mumbled after a dozen hands without a pot.

"That's the way luck runs in an honest game," the Fiddler observed.

"You tryn' say somethin'?" the Kid asked belligerently.

"Never sit in a game with a man you don't know," the Fiddler said, winking at the Preacher as he curled the nonexistent points of his mustache.

Jake laughed at the remark and the gesture and curled the ends of his own magnificent adornment.

Jake and Mac drank almost as heavily as the Kid but they held their liquor better. The Preacher drank moderately but not so reasonably as he thought. The Fiddler emptied most of his whiskey in the Preacher's cup while he and the others were studying their cards.

By midnight, cards were spilling from the deck when the dealer shuffled and the players were nodding between hands. The Preacher shook his old gray head, looking baffled. "I'm drunk as a boiled owl," he muttered.

"You, too?" the Fiddler asked and swayed a bit as he reached uncertainly for the jug.

The Kid had gone to sleep with his head on folded arms. Jake's and Mac's heads had fallen on their chests.

"Enough!" the Preacher proclaimed.

"A nightcap?" the Fiddler suggested.

"Why not?" the Preacher agreed with a half smile.

"None for the Kid," the Fiddler said and shook Jake and Mac to awaken them.

When they'd downed the last cup, the Fiddler included, his first real drink of the night, Jake and Mac carried the Kid to his blanket and propped his head on the saddle. They laid down fully clothed and lifted blankets over their boots. The Preacher pulled off his boots and socks. The Fiddler left one lantern turned low and removed his shirt and boots but left his socks on. His four companions were deep in noisy sleep within five minutes but he waited until the clock showed twelve-thirty before he moved. He removed the makings from the tobacco pouch, took the second lantern, but did not light it until he'd placed it within the small tunnel. Then he squeezed in following the light down to the granite slab. He reopened some of the cuts on his chest when he burrowed under it.

The account Boots had given him about Eph and the mortgage had angered him more than he'd shown. He was convinced Eph had killed Eli for the property. He did not think Eph knew about the cavern or the gold but he did think Eli's unguarded remark had alerted him and drawn his attention to other possibilities on the bench. He detested Eph as he'd despise anyone who'd shoot a man in the back, particularly when that man was his brother; but more, he was enraged at the way Eph was cheating Boots. He did not yet know how, but he meant to see that Eph paid the full price for murder. First, however, Boots was going to redeem the mortgage and claim the property.

The glittering, creamy-white quartz cave with its bubbling spring and dark vein of gold above was as awesome as he recalled it. This must have been the sacred source of precious metal for idols and amulets. He took a handful of gold shavings from the buckskin bag and placed them in the pouch. He did not know the value of gold but the weight seemed slight so he added a second and third hand-

ful for good measure until the pouch had heft. He hoped
he'd taken enough.

The Fiddler left the large buckskin bag in the quartz
chamber. It was the only safe place he knew. He crawled
back to the cavern without delay, extinguishing the lantern
before he pulled himself out of the tunnel.

He replaced the lantern and softly in his stockinged feet
paused at each of his companions. Each was snoring lustily.
He did not think one of them had stirred.

He did not sleep well that night.

It was six o'clock when he quit his fitful pallet and went
to the stream. The others remained in profound stupor. He
started coffee over a fat lamp and when he'd scrubbed and
dressed, he fried bacon and eggs. He'd finished breakfast
and was waiting for the coffee to boil when three raps
echoed down the tunnel. It was just seven o'clock. He
buckled on his gunbelt and hurried to the panel wondering
what was wrong.

Boots was standing outside the stall, feet apart, fists
thrust in the pockets of her dungarees. She was wearing a
yellow shirt that fit her and a teasing smile.

"Oh!" she exclaimed, feigning astonishment. "I was
looking for the Fiddler."

"They took him to the lockup," he said. The more he
saw, and was with, and talked with this woman, the better
he liked her.

"No they didn't, Franklyn Bye, and they won't!" she
said emphatically. "They've given up."

"How do you know that at seven o'clock in the morning?" he asked skeptically.

"The marshal and the posse rode by half an hour ago,
heading for town." Her eyes shone. "And they didn't have
the Fiddler with them."

"I knew the marshal was discouraged but I thought he might give it another day," he said.

"I think the posse quit," she said. "Can a girl ask a favor?"

"It's yours without the asking, Boots."

"Had your breakfast?"

"Just finished." He was sorry he had.

"Then come to the porch for a cup of coffee. There's a breeze today and it's passing comfortable."

"That's a favor?"

She smiled slyly. "Bring your fiddle."

He hesitated only briefly. If the posse had returned, there should be no risk, and anyway, he doubted the sound would carry two miles to the road. "Command performance!" He bowed and turned to the stall.

"Oh tell the others the coffee pot's on," she added in an unenthusiastic afterthrought.

He grinned. "I'm afraid they'll have to decline the invitation. They painted their tonsils last night."

"Oh what a shame!" she said and slumped dejectedly away.

It was a pleasant summer morning, still warm but the west wind came from high places and was refreshing and scented of pine. It was strange to the Fiddler, not feeling long hair blowing about his face. It gave him a curious sense of freedom.

Boots had brought out a spool-backed straight chair. Two cups of coffee were on an upended cartridge case between it and the rocker.

"Where do all the cartridge cases come from?" He took the straight chair and placed the fiddle and bow on the floor.

"Eli collected them in town for the range," she said, taking the rocker. "I still do. Firewood's scarce."

He wanted a cigarette with his coffee but after her experience the night before, he hesitated. "All right if I smoke? If I don't leave the makings behind?"

"Of course. Milk or sugar?"

"No, thank you." He took out the cloth bag of tobacco.

"Where's the leather pouch?" she asked.

He felt its solid weight in his hip pocket. "I'm going to fill it with fresh tobacco. Wanted to finish this first."

She fell silent and serious and a cloud passed over her eyes. "I found the bank papers after you left last night. The mortgage falls due next week."

He wanted to tell her not to worry but was reluctant to mention the gold. He wasn't sure he'd ever tell her about it. "Is an extension possible?"

"The bank gave Eli one extension. I don't think they'd hold still for another. It would make no difference, now that Eph holds the option." She shrugged and put on a brave face. "I shouldn't have mentioned it."

She was unhappy and he wanted to cheer her. "The mortgage will be paid, Boots. I promise you that. You'll keep the Diamond C."

"You're not going to rob a bank, Frank," she said sharply. "I won't have you even thinking like that. I'd never accept stolen money."

He laughed. "I know that. Anyway, that life is over."

Sunshine banished her troubles, and her face was happy again. "You really mean it?"

"Yes, Boots. Final decision." He grinned. "I'll sell the Stradivarius." He picked up the fiddle.

"Play me a gay tune."

He shredded the cigarette, threw the tobacco to the

wind, checked his shirt pocket to be sure the makings were there, and made a show of tuning the strings. "Don't know whether I'll be able to play with short hair," he said, tapping his foot. He put the fiddle to his chest, ran the bow across the strings in a few preliminary flourishes and, head swaying in tempo, started a lively tune, "Turkey in the Straw."

A few miles away, Marshal Cyrus Fargo was riding north once more, this time with his deputy, Bart Axelrod. Both men were saddle-weary and road-strained. Bart's chest was heaving and he blew out his parched lips each time he expelled a breath. He'd been in the saddle for most of thirty-six hours and was angry. When he'd returned disheartened that morning with a posse that refused to go farther, Fargo had ordered him back in the saddle. Now on the road again, he turned his reddened eyes to the marshal, whose face was engraved with the lines of defeat.

"Cyrus, I tell you, it's no use," he complained. "You been through this country two, three times and I done the same to the south. Every ranchhouse, barn, and pigpen has been turned inside and out and every haystack, gulley, and stand of trees upside down. There ain't a inch of ground we ain't covered. The men all got tired and quit. What in tarnation hell's the sense of this one more time?"

The face Fargo turned to the deputy was forbidding. "It's a feeling I got that they're right here under our nose. When you been a lawman long as I have, Bart, you'll learn to respect that feeling. It's an instinct you got to regard. You come to sense things without knowing why. Someplace along in here there's something that's not right. I haven't seen it yet but I will. That's why we're going over this ground one last time."

Bart had it up to his craw. "Where you aim to look for what's out of kilter? How you going to look for something when you don't know what it is?"

"It'll come, Bart, it'll show itself." Fargo's eyes half closed as he concentrated. In a low, toneless voice that sounded like a chant, he reviewed his thoughts to Bart, who half-dozed. "We know those ponies were stolen and hidden to deceive us. They meant for us to think they were afoot. That meant they had horses."

"Sure they had horses," Bart said, letting the marshal hear he was peeved. "That's why it's damned nonsense to keep looking around here. They're over the hill in California by now."

"That's what they want us to think, same as they wanted us to think they were on foot, maybe holed up in town. They're hiding out somewhere along here." The marshal looked to the west and the east.

"That don't make sense, Cyrus," Bart said from a throat so dry his words scratched. "They put us off-trail to gain time for a day or two head start. They got away while we fooled around town. Why would they stay here even if they could?"

"They're waiting for us to give up," Fargo reasoned. "When we quit looking for them, they'll go."

"Bosh!" Bart said with great feeling. "That don't hold water at all."

"Yes it does," Fargo asserted. "If they'd ridden straight off like you say, they'd be bound to leave a trail somewhere we could follow. There'd be sign we could read. But they're sitting tight somewhere and we've got nothing to go on. When we aren't looking any longer, they can ride where they want and not even be careful."

"You sure they got horses?" Bart asked craftily.

"Got to have horses." The marshal was positive.

"How'd they hide horses without leaving sign?" Bart asked triumphantly.

Fargo's glance was stormy and Bart retreated into sullen silence.

They had ridden without speaking when Fargo reined up with a jerk that pulled the mustang's head high. "Bart! Hear that? It's the Fiddler a-playing."

"I don't hear nothing but the sound of your voice," Bart said, thoroughly disgusted.

The marshal held his head to the side, listening intently, and considered their surroundings. They were at the foot of the slope below the Diamond C. "It's stopped now. It was coming from the Widow Carrington's."

"You couldn't hear anything from up there, way down here," Bart said, completely out of sorts.

The marshal considered. "There's a good west wind. It could carry sound like a fiddle makes. It had to come from the widow's." His eyes were bright with fierce satisfaction. "I had my doubts about her from the start."

"The widow!" Bart was appalled. "That woman wouldn't harm a cinch bug."

"Exactly," the marshal cried. "That fits in with the rest of their plan. We wouldn't suspect her. I distinctly heard the Fiddler playing a hoedown." He kicked his horse up the slope at a gallop.

Bart followed in dispirited resignation. He was sick at heart and ashamed of the marshal and himself when he saw the small, sweaty figure of the widow in work pants and shirt come from the garden dragging a hoe.

"What is it this time, Marshal?" she asked in a tone so cold it penetrated Bart's bones.

The mustang reared at the tight fist on the reins, and

Fargo was out of the saddle before the horse found four legs. "Where is he?" He confronted the widow brutally.

"Where is who?" Each word was an icicle that pierced Bart's chest. She was a pillar of ice. He wanted to rein about and leave the marshal to face her alone.

"The Fiddler!" Fargo lost all control and bellowed. "I heard him playing a shindig clear down to the road."

Bart looked away, about the small place. All seemed serene. A black and white dog came to the widow's side and growled at the marshal. "I didn't hear anything, ma'am," he felt obliged to say. He wanted a drink of water but felt he couldn't ask.

The widow was frozen fury. "Marshal Fargo," she said contemptuously, "I have had enough of your accusations." She returned to the parched garden and resumed hoeing her vegetables.

"Cyrus, there's nobody here," Bart pleaded. "You're making fools out of us. Let's go."

"Part of the plan," Fargo said knowingly. "All part of the plan. Come along, Bart. We'll ferret him out."

He led Bart through the house and the barn, probed the hay in the loft, and put a fork in the dirt in each empty stall. He did not examine the double stall where a cow and calf were tethered.

"Where could anyone hide?" Bart asked when they'd gone back outside and he'd had a drink at the pump.

"Up there," the marshal shouted wildly and fired five rounds into the high branches of a ponderosa pine. No one cried out. No one fell down.

"I'm leaving," Bart said at that antic and stepped into the saddle. "This is starting to get to you."

That stopped the marshal dead in his tracks, at the side of the porch where he was trying to find a crawl space under the six-inch-high floor. When he walked to the mustang his face was the color of cold ashes. He mounted and walked the horse down the slope without looking back.

They rode in silence, Fargo slumped in the saddle and head bowed, for more than a mile before Bart spoke. "It ain't that you're out of your mind, Cyrus. You got so hogtied on this Fiddler breaking your jail and so dead set on taking him back, you're hearing things in your head that ain't even there. It's worked on you so hard you're obsessed. What you need is a rest."

"I suppose you're right," Fargo said meekly. It was the first time he'd ever agreed with Bart on anything.

XI

The Fiddler had been performing a porch-rattling jig to his own accompaniment when Boots had interrupted him. "Frank! Two riders have stopped and they're looking this way."

Down the rock-strewn clay slope, he saw one of the riders start up the rutted trail. The wind had betrayed him. With the sun in the east at the rider's back, there was no way to get to the barn without being seen unless he snaked on his belly, and he didn't think there was time for that. His mind turned over options as he took the chair and his cup to the kitchen. Boots hurried in with the cartridge case and her cup.

"Are you going to try out your disguise?" She smiled but her eyes were uncertain. She rinsed out the cups and put them behind a red and white gingham curtain in the cupboard.

"Not now. Even Franklyn Bye would be too hard to explain at this time of the morning." He was looking swiftly around the kitchen, at the table, on the shelves. "Besides, it would spoil other plans. Have you a pencil? A piece of chalk? Anything to write with?"

She didn't ask why. She took a stick of charcoal from a drawer in the cupboard. "Will this do?"

"Fine." He took it, fiddle, and bow and started out.

"Where are you going to hide?"

"You'll see." He laughed. "Don't worry, Boots. Whoever they are, they'll never find me. Don't worry. Get out to the garden and hoe."

Now he heard Boots call, "You can come out. They've started for town."

He opened the door and stepped from the small privy at the back side of the house. She was waiting for him a few yards away, one eyebrow cocked above a speculative eye.

"How could you be sure he wouldn't look for you in there?" she asked and bubbled with laughter.

"You live here alone and it's your private place." He closed the door. "I added that for insurance."

The charcoal script on the door read: *Women Only.*

"I know. I saw it from the garden and it almost ruined my act." She held her ribs and bent in laughter. When she straightened, the urchin look was back on her face. "The marshal saw it, too, and didn't look that way again. But suppose he had tried the door?"

"No gentleman would invade such a privileged place," he said and put a shocked look on his face.

"You did," she said pointedly.

"The answer is obvious."

"But suppose he had," she persisted.

"The door was hooked from inside. If he'd rattled it, I'd have screamed in my best falsetto and left the rest to you." He grinned and added, "I have great confidence in you. I heard most of what went on."

He took her arm and they started for the porch. "That poor, frustrated man," she said. "I almost felt sorry for him."

"He's frustrated because he hasn't been able to string up the Fiddler," he said. "I'll wash the door."

"Never. I'll take that door with me when I leave." She

looked at him with a rogue smile. "You could at least have written *Ladies*."

"If I'd misspelled it, he'd have stormed right into the *Laddies*."

Boots had brought back the chair and case and refilled the cups. The Fiddler laid his fiddle and bow on the floor. "He'll never be back," he said, sitting and rolling a cigarette.

"No. I think the ordeal is over." The laughter left her eyes and she said seriously, "What are your plans now, Frank?"

"I'll ride to Carson City tomorrow to buy some horses," he said carefully. "Now is the best time to leave, when they've quit and aren't looking for us."

He could see she was upset but she said, "You can have the mustangs and Milford has his roan. You'll need only two."

"I told you not to worry about the mortgage," he said. "The mustangs wouldn't bring enough to make any difference."

"I said you could *have* them." Her words were angry because she was disturbed, he knew.

He shook his head. "Thanks, Boots. We'd intended to buy them but after the fuss with the marshal, riding your brand is a risk we can't allow you to take. If we run into trouble, your mustangs would be hard to explain. We'll leave the Preacher's roan behind with you, too. It wears your brand now."

"And from here?" There was no spirit left in her voice.

"Wyoming Territory."

She looked dismayed. "You said you were through with the outlaw life, Frank."

"I am." He wanted to tell her more but he was plagued with uncertainty. Too many things remained to be settled.

"I'll leave the band when I know they've reached safety."
She smiled, faintly hopeful. "You'll come back?"

"I can't answer that, Boots," he said gently. A little
hurt now was better than heartbreak later. "A man doesn't
make promises unless he knows he can keep them. Please
don't question me too closely."

For the flicker of an eyelash, a look of such abject hope-
lessness was in her eyes that he wanted to take her in his
arms but he knew he could not reassure her. Then the
gamin-eyed urchin was smiling at him. "I've an idea,
Frank."

"I like your ideas, and you have them by the wagon-
load." He matched her courage with a smile of his own.

"Cowboy clothes don't go with the way you look now,"
she said. What she had in mind seemed to please and ani-
mate her. "You need clothes to fit Franklyn Bye. They'll
change your appearance as much as your mustache and hair.
Eli was about your size. I've a dark suit of his, dark hat,
and boots. It seemed foolish to bury good clothes in a pine
box."

A quizzical smile tugged at his lips. A change of clothing
would help, he admitted, but he was astonished at the cas-
ual regard she seemed to have for her late murdered husband. "What did you bury him in? Bib overalls?"

"Long underwear," she said with no note of apology.

He couldn't stifle his laugh and she joined him.

"What difference could it possibly make to anyone?" she
asked logically. "I'll air the suit and sponge and press it."
She frowned as if she were puzzling some thought. "What
was it you said about irrigating the bench? How could that
be done? That's just a small stream through the pasture."

"Come on, I'll show you." She started to protest and he
said quickly, "That garden's been hoed enough to last all

summer. Won't matter anyway, if we don't get rain soon. Put the fiddle and bow under your bed and we'll take a walk."

He carried the chair and cartridge case to the kitchen. She rinsed the cups and put them away.

Heidi ranged ahead in the dry graze pouncing after grasshoppers. The sky was an unblemished blue tint, the sun bright and warm, and the breeze scented with pine resin. The hills rose in waves to the west until in the far distance they touched the mountains. To the east, the land stretched out in an endless tawny carpet. It was a good place here on the bench, a quiet place where love could live. He felt a pressure on his fingers and was surprised to find he was holding her hand.

He took her to the side of the hill where the clear-water stream poured onto the land in an unending flow.

"There's some slope, even here on the bench," he pointed out. "I'd terrace it in two or three levels."

"That would be an enormous undertaking," she objected.

"Not so much of a job as you'd think," he said. The bench was about a mile long and a half-mile wide. "No more than plowing a large field. Nothing a man with a team couldn't handle." He considered the lay of the land. "Right here, where we're standing, I'd scoop out this area, build an earth dam with a sluice gate to control the water level. There would be channels off the pool with gates to control the flow to the terraces so you could shut the water on and off as it was needed." He laughed. "You could have ducks and geese on the pond."

"You make it sound wonderful," she exclaimed, looking about as if she were seeing the fowl paddling in the water. "But so complicated. It would take an engineer."

"Nonsense," he said, laughing. "It's an irrigation method that's been used for thousands of years by peasants in China, India, even ancient Egypt. When you have a good source of water, as you do here, all that's needed is labor."

"Maybe," she said doubtfully.

He looked at the dry, tannish earth of her garden plot, which started some three hundred yards from where they were standing. The land fell gently to it. "Your garden could easily be irrigated. All that's needed is a gate here at the stream and a small channel to it." He considered the distance a moment longer. "It's no job at all. We'll do it."

She seemed bewildered. She said slowly, "You mean you are going to irrigate the garden for me?"

"Of course." He chuckled. "I'll roust the survivors. Do them good to sweat out the whiskey. We'll have your garden irrigated by evening."

"I do not believe this," she said and she was unusually quiet on the walk to the house. When she brought the fiddle and bow to him on the porch, she said, "I don't think irrigation was what Eli had in mind when he made that remark about money to Eph. The way you've explained it, I can understand how it could be done. I think it would work. But Eli didn't have much imagination. He only saw what was already there. He could not have comprehended the things you've told me. The remark he made to Eph was nothing but pretense."

The image she had created of Eli in all their conversations and her attitude toward him troubled the Fiddler. He did not understand how a woman with Boots' sense of humor, intelligence, and spirit could have tolerated such a person. "It's personal and I've no right to ask," he said quietly, "but how did you come to marry him?"

"I don't mind." Her slight shrug indicated it was a matter she'd dismissed long ago. "He was a friend of my father's in Illinois. My mother and father died from diphtheria. They called it putrid sore throat where we lived. We had nothing. My father was a wheelwright. No family except Milford and he was somewhere in the West. Before my father died, he gave me to Eli to care for me. I was fifteen. We were married and came out here in a covered wagon. He was like a father to me. I never was his wife."

The Fiddler thought he heard a sob catch in her throat as she turned quickly and went into the house.

Only the Kid objected to the day's work the Fiddler laid before the band. The idea excited the Preacher. "She can make this the most profitable farm in Nevada," he said.

The Fiddler did not tell him the mortgage was due the next week and Eph held an option.

Jake and Mac seemed to welcome the opportunity to get outdoors and do some manual labor.

"Hey friend," the Kid protested, "I got this sledge hammering in my head. Leave me alone. Let me stay here and sleep."

"You need fresh air," the Fiddler said. "Can you climb the ponderosa?"

"I think I might do that," the Kid said uncertainly.

"All right. Don't go to sleep and fall off the branch."

Heidi was waiting for the Preacher when the band left the barn. The Kid painfully climbed the pine, and the Fiddler told the others to simply lie down when someone passed on the road. "We won't have visitors," he assured them.

The Fiddler chopped stakes from a cartridge case and, with the Preacher holding them and a ball of baling twine, lacking a transit, ran a line-of-sight survey and established a rough five-degree grade from the garden to the stream. While Jake and Mac dug a channel one foot wide, the Preacher and he started work on the sluice gate. He excavated a horizontal trench well below the depth the channel was to take and hammered together grooved uprights for the gate supports. The gate was fashioned from cartridge cases with a heavy iron stave at the bottom, both for weight and to bite into the earth and seal the channel when the ditch was not in operation. When the gate was in place, he ran a rope from it over a pulley he'd found in the barn and attached to one of the supports so Boots could operate it.

"Where did you study engineering, Frank?" the Preacher asked casually.

"VMI," the Fiddler answered without thinking.

"Virginia Military Institute," the Preacher said reflectively. "I thought something like that. I shouldn't have asked but I couldn't help it."

The Fiddler chuckled. "It's all right, Milford. I'm sure it won't go any farther. I know something of your background, too."

About the middle of the afternoon, Boots brought out a bucket of cold water and beef sandwiches. "Come back to the house with me, Frank," she said.

The Preacher was wearing a pleased smile as they walked away together.

Boots had Eli's clothes cleaned, pressed, and laid out on her bed for him. He told himself it was all right, she had no other place to put them, but it gave him a strange feeling to be in the bedroom with her. There were twelve-inch black boots like the Preacher wore. They conformed to the sole of his own boots. There was a flat-crowned black hat, seldom worn. It fit. There was a white shirt and black string tie. The black broadcloth suit had a frock coat. He put his arms in the sleeves, and the coat fit across the shoulders.

Without thinking, because he wanted to, he impulsively kissed her.

Neither of them spoke. Her hand rested lightly on his arm. Her eyes were large and solemn. Abruptly, she said, "Go try them on."

He breathed deeply. "I don't know, Boots. I'm still the Fiddler inside."

"Thank heavens!" she said and a little color came into her cheeks.

He shouldn't have kissed her, he thought as he changed clothes in the cavern. He was angry with himself. He had been careful to avoid anything that might be misinterpreted. If things didn't go right, if he didn't return, he wanted no tears. There had been little joy in her life. He buckled his gunbelt under the frock coat and returned to the house in his somber attire.

"Franklyn Bye!" There was high color now in Boots' face. Her eyes were neither impish nor solemn. They were happy eyes. "But should you be wearing your gun?"

He felt strange, inside as well as out. "I'm not exactly a parson," he said.

"You don't look like a parson," she said. "You're a gentleman of obvious means."

He thought of the pouch of gold he'd tucked in his hip pocket, the bag of gold in the quartz cave, and the vein above the spring, and couldn't help smiling.

"Halloo, the house!" the Preacher called from the gate.

Boots and the Fiddler stepped from the porch and looked up the newly dug ditch. Jake and Mac had reached the sluice gate and were ready to cut through to the stream.

They were standing with the Preacher and all three were staring at Fiddler. He laughed. He knew it was only because he was with Boots that they hadn't reached for the guns.

"Come down, Kid," the Fiddler shouted to the branches.

There was no response and Boots and he walked toward the gate.

Mac was laughing. "You're prettier 'n' a spotted dog under a red wagon," he said.

"He ain't pretty," Jake growled, curling the end of his mustache. "I seen plenty of killers dressed like that."

"And parsons," the Preacher said. He was smiling broadly. "You could confront the marshal and he'd not have the slightest misgivings. You look solid and substantial."

"Boots said something like that," the Fiddler recalled.

"I don't feel easy with him around," Jake muttered.

"We're ready to try it," the Preacher said.

Jake and Mac cut away the foot of earth that separated the gate from the stream. Water rushed in to the gate.

"See if you can operate it, Boots," the Fiddler said.

She grasped the rope with both hands and pulled. The gate lifted and water filled the channel and started toward the garden. Boots still clung to the line.

"We forgot one thing, Preacher," the Fiddler said. He pounded a stake into the ground. "Wrap the rope around that and let go," he told her.

A trench had been dug horizontally across the back of the garden. The water quickly filled it and ran down between the rows.

"It's too fast," he told Boots. "Lower the gate halfway and hold the rope there."

The water still overflowed the ditch and rows.

"Another quarter." He watched closely. "A few more inches."

When the flow was regulated so only a trickle ran into the garden rows, he told her to tie the line and leave it.

"I'll be back this evening to check it," he said. "With the earth so dry, you'll have to let it in easy for a while or the water will just spill out."

"I can almost see the corn growing," Boots said.

The Preacher picked up the ax and hammer. "I think we'd better get back to the cavern. We missed breakfast and dinner. You coming, Frank?"

"Yes," the Fiddler said, taking Boots' arm. "Go on ahead. I'll shake the Kid out of the tree and be there in a few minutes."

Jake and Mac picked up their spades and went with the Preacher. The Fiddler pelted the branches with clods of dirt until the Kid skinned down, wild-eyed and swearing.

"Easy, boy," the Fiddler said sharply. "Get into the cave."

The Kid turned on him savagely and became aware of his dress for the first time. He let out a yip and said derisively, "Forgive me, *padre*. I have sinned." He ran to the barn, hooting and howling all the way.

Boots had ignored the Kid. She had walked to the edge of the garden and stood there watching the earth darken with moisture. The Fiddler went to her.

"It's a miracle," she said in a wondering voice, "but it makes me a little sad."

"Why?" he asked, taken aback.

"To think Eph should get the property, and now this, too," she said quietly.

The Fiddler took her by the shoulders and faced her to him. Her eyes were forlorn. It was difficult to restrain himself from kissing her again. "I didn't do this for Eph," he said firmly. "Believe me, Boots. I'll take care of Eph."

XII

The Kid had found the whiskey jug and was pouring himself a cupful when the Fiddler strode into the cavern. The Preacher was at the stream with the coffee pot, and Jake and Mac were stretched out on the blankets. The Fiddler lifted the crock from the Kid's fist.

"Drink that cup if you need a hair of the dog," he said roughly. "But no more. We're riding out tomorrow night and I don't want you falling out of your saddle."

The Kid glowered in sullen silence and took the cup to the end of the table. The Fiddler carried the whiskey to the Preacher.

"Keep your eye on the whiskey and the Kid," the Fiddler warned him. "He's got a cup now. No more."

The Preacher frowned. "I'm sorry about that, Frank. I thought I'd stashed it."

"When things are cooking, I'd like to talk with you."

The Preacher smiled. "The Kid can do the cooking. It'll slow down his drinking."

When the Kid had taken over at the fat lamps, the Preacher splashed out some whiskey for the Fiddler and himself and they sat at the table. "What's on your mind, Frank?" the Preacher asked amiably.

"I'm going to have to buy five horses," the Fiddler said and told him why. "How much do we have in the poke?"

"About five hundred dollars," the Preacher told him.

"Let me have two hundred and fifty. We don't want nags. I'll leave at sunup."

The Preacher was thoughtful. "Five horses is going to make quite a string. Want me to ride along?"

"I'd like that." The Preacher and he always had been congenial but with the business the Fiddler was going to transact, he could not risk the Preacher's company. "The only thing is, that would put two Diamond C horses on the road. Even one will be conspicuous. I'd like to take the roan."

"Of course, Frank." The Preacher's eyes narrowed and he put some furrows in his forehead. "Better not take the road. Use the back trail, the same one we came over. You'll pick up another above it just before you reach town."

"I was going to ask. Owlhoot?"

"The same."

"That helps," he said and grinned. "I'll try to be back before noon. I'll leave the horses in the stand of pine until we're ready to leave. Keep the men busy inside, especially the Kid. They can divide up the things we'll take and make up the rolls. Is there anything we need?"

The Preacher chuckled. "A bottle of Double Stamp for you and me but keep it hidden."

"Bet your boots," the Fiddler said and laughed. "I'll tell Boots not to signal in the morning."

"You and my niece seem to hit it off pretty well," the Preacher said with a satisfied smile.

"I wish things were different," the Fiddler said frankly.

The Preacher was direct. "They are, Franklyn Bye."

"If that works out," the Fiddler said cautiously. "I've got to try it out first. I won't do anything that might hurt her."

"It will work," the Preacher said confidently. "Look at

you now. I have to keep reminding myself that you're the Fiddler, not a stranger. Don't leave with us. Stay with her."

"This was my intention and I want to see the end of it, Preacher." The Fiddler decided to tell the Preacher his plan. "The stranger is part of it. That's the way I want to return to Virginia City. When the band is well on the way, I'll come back. Before I see Boots again, I'll make my test. If I pass, I'll contrive to meet her in some public way that is convincing to the town. This has to look right for her." He hesitated and smiled ruefully. "I haven't talked with Boots about this. I'm being presumptuous. I don't know she'll have me."

The Preacher laughed softly. "I've seen the two of you together. She'll be waiting for you. You have my blessing."

The Kid's supper consisted of beans, sowbelly, and cold biscuits. The Fiddler turned his plate over and drank a cup of coffee. When he finished a cigarette, he slapped on the flat-crowned black hat.

The cup of whiskey was working in the Kid and he said, "Remember, friend, I told you what I'd do if you didn't stay away from that mare."

The Preacher backhanded him from his perch on a case.

The Fiddler had not changed into his own clothes. He wanted to accustom himself to the frock coat and collar so he felt at ease and he wanted to please Boots although he still wore his gun.

When he went out of the barn into the sunset, she was walking along the edge of the garden, still wearing dungarees and yellow shirt. She paused at each row to examine the soil the moisture was darkening. When she heard him, she turned, a full, warm smile on her lips.

"Hello, Frank," she greeted him, voice richly intimate. The things it implied gave his heart a tug.

"Evening, Boots," he said with a slow smile. "How does your garden grow?"

"It will now." She sounded breathless.

He looked up a row of carrots. The water was standing. "It's seeping in. The ground was very dry. I think I'd leave the gate open all night and close it in the morning. That's the time to irrigate, at night. Open the gate a few inches again tomorrow night."

"You won't be here then?"

"We'll be packing up and saddling, getting ready to ride as soon as it's dark."

"It's going to be lonely." She put her arm through his and added, "Until you come back."

He hadn't said he'd return. He'd told her he'd make no promises. He'd tried to be careful. He shouldn't have kissed her.

They walked to the porch. The sun was sinking behind the far hills in a splendid blaze and it was warm. The breeze that had fanned the day had gone away and it was very still.

"Wonder why a man wears such an outfit," he grumbled, unbuttoning the frock coat and removing the hat before sitting on the edge of the porch.

"To hide a big belly," she said, sitting beside him, "or a fat rump."

He looked at her sternly but a smile pulled at his lips. "The anatomical parts you mention are not discussed in mixed company."

"Oh balderdash!" she said with feeling.

"And that from the lips of a lady." He looked at her fondly. "Everything about you surprises me. How did you come by your education?"

"Oh—" She shrugged slightly. "My mother, I guess.

She'd been a schoolmarm. You know: one room, all the grades through six. She taught me to read before I was five. I've always read every book I could beg. Still do. About the only things I own are my books. And Heidi."

"Where is Heidi?" he asked, looking around.

"In the kitchen, eating. I keep her in the house with me for company. Would you like something to eat? Some coffee?"

"Thank you, no." He took her hand. It was hard, work-worn, and rough, but she did not pull it away. "It's pleasant just sitting here and talking. I can't talk when I eat."

The sun had set and a pale twilight was creeping over the land. There was a hush that was lulling. He sat back, bracing himself on one hand and closing his eyes. And heard horseshoes striking stone from the direction of the gulley.

He shook his head and picked up his hat. "I guess I'd better leave while I can," he said with weary resignation.

She clung to his hand. "No, Frank, stay. I can't guess who it might be. I don't have visitors and it's not the marshal, I'm sure. Go into the kitchen. I'll send him away. If it sounds threatening, you can go out the bedroom window."

He stepped inside. Heidi lifted her head from her pan of scraps long enough to wag her tail and resumed her supper. He glanced around quickly. The kitchen was too open but the bedroom was in shadow and he went into it where he could sit on the floor by the bed and watch through the door. He heard the rocking chair begin to teeter forth and back.

A lone rider on a great black horse pawed from the embankment onto the lip of the bench. As he approached the house, the Fiddler saw that the rider was dressed much the same as he, in flat-crowned black hat and dark frock coat.

The coat was opened and revealed crisscrossed belts and two guns. Jake's reference to a gunman dressed in this fashion flashed across his mind and he shifted to a crouch. The rider reined up near the house. His dark eyes in a long, gaunt face burned like a cat's. Boots apparently recognized him because she went out to him.

"Eph!" she exclaimed.

A cold, deadly calm steadied the Fiddler's hand on his gun. This was the rustler and murderer who plundered widows.

"Evening, Boots," Eph said. His voice was harsh, remote, yet insinuating. "Thought I'd best ride by to see if you was safe."

"Why wouldn't I be?" she asked curtly and, without enthusiasm, invited, "Step down and sit on the porch until it cools off."

"Thank you," Eph said, but the acknowledgment was neither friendly nor courteous. He ground-reined the horse and stepped onto the porch ahead of Boots.

"I'll get a chair from the kitchen," she murmured.

Eph crossed the floor and the Fiddler heard him take the rocking chair. He stepped from the bedroom to reassure her. Her face looked pale and drawn. He pointed in Eph's direction and shook his head, emphatically, No! She nodded her head in grave agreement and returned to the porch with the chair. Heidi went with her, growling.

"What is it, Eph?" the Fiddler heard Boots ask coolly. "It wasn't concern for my safety that brought you out here."

"If it's direct talk you're wanting, you'll get it," Eph snapped. "Come Tuesday, the mortgage is due. You fixed to meet it?"

"This isn't Tuesday," Boots said.

"What difference a day or two? If you ain't got the money now, you won't have it then." There was a pause and the night was so still the Fiddler could hear Eph strike a lucifer. "We'll go to the bank tomorrow, pay off the mortgage, and sign over the deed. I'll stay with you tonight."

The Fiddler fought back the fury that inflamed him. For the second time in as many days, he wanted to kill a man.

"You had better leave now." Her voice was scornful.

"Settle down, Widow Carrington," Eph said condescendingly. "We'll do this my way. I want this took care of tomorrow. I got other business next week. Far as staying here's concerned, that's just ordinary hospitality to a relative."

"You're no relation of mine," she flared.

The Fiddler had his gun in his hand. There'd be no question of draw. He'd fire first.

"I like a woman with spirit," Eph said with a sneer the Fiddler could feel. "Don't put on no airs. You been bedded before."

The Fiddler was moving in the kitchen when he heard someone brush along the house under the window. He stepped quickly back and saw the Kid crouched at the corner and the bright blade of a knife in his hand.

The Fiddler went swiftly to the kitchen door. Abruptly, Eph was out of the chair, wheeling and drawing both guns. The Fiddler shifted his grip to the muzzle of his gun. He charged across the porch and clubbed Eph at the base of the skull. The man crumpled slowly and his guns crashed to the floor.

"Kid!" the Fiddler thundered. "Get up here fast. You've put all our necks in a noose."

The Kid slunk from the side of the house, knife still in hand.

"Is this what you mean by taking care of Eph?" Boots cried agonizingly. "You're no better than he."

"The Kid came here to kill me," the Fiddler told her sharply.

"I came to save you from the Fiddler," the Kid said, sheathing his knife. "Who is he?"

"The hangman, if we don't move fast," the Fiddler said, picking up Eph's guns. He tucked them in his gunbelt. "Boots, get some rope and a sheet."

She ran to the kitchen without saying more.

"You damned idiot," the Fiddler raged at the Kid. "Now we have hell to pay."

"Why don't we just kill him?" the Kid asked indifferently.

The Fiddler smashed his fist in the Kid's face and picked him off the floor. Blood began to ooze at the corners of his mouth. "It isn't that simple." He threw him against the wall and the Kid slid down. "Do what I tell you. Do it fast and do it right. Maybe I still can save your hide."

Boots brought rope and a sheet.

"Get up!" the Fiddler ordered the Kid. "Give me your knife."

The Kid pushed himself up. Now he seemed more frightened than angry.

The Fiddler sliced off a length of rope and handed it to the Kid.

"Pull off his boots, cross his ankles, and tie them fast, around and in between." The Fiddler had Eph's wrists behind his back and was looping the rope around them, crossed.

"I know how to tie a man up so he can't get away," the Kid said defensively.

"Do it then!" To Boots he said, "Rip that sheet in strips. We'll hogtie him later. First we'll gag and blindfold him." He stuffed a wadding of sheet into Eph's mouth and bound a strip tightly about it. When he'd secured a blindfold over his eyes, he wrapped strips of cloth tightly about Eph's face, leaving only an opening for his nostrils, and then more strips from under Eph's chin to the top of his head and around his neck. When the Fiddler was through, Eph looked like a mummy.

"We don't touch anything he has, including money," the Fiddler commanded. "And we don't talk from now on within earshot. We don't know when he'll come to. Help me carry him away from the porch and go get the Preacher, Jake, and Mac."

Eph still was unconscious when they dropped him far out toward the embankment. The Fiddler went back for Eph's hat and boots while the Kid ran for the others.

"This is terrible," Boots whispered in the kitchen, where she'd lighted a lamp.

"Yes it is," the Fiddler agreed tightly. "For all of us, especially you."

"What will you do?"

"I don't know." The only thought he'd had was to immobilize Eph to gain time to think. "I was ready to kill him before the Kid mistook him for me. Maybe something will come to mind but I'll still kill him if I have to."

She bit her lip but nodded her head in silent agreement.

The Kid brought the others back at a run. The Preacher's eyes were blazing. "What—"

The Fiddler shook his head, beckoned Boots, and led them into the barn.

"The Kid's put us all in a jam." He glanced contemptuously at the Kid. "That's Eph, Eli's brother, bound up out there. When the Kid jumped him thinking it was me, I had to slug Eph to keep him from killing the Kid."

Jake's eyes burned when he glanced at the Kid. "You should of let him do it. It would of saved a lot of trouble."

"We couldn't leave the Kid's body on Boots' doorstep," the Fiddler pointed out. "How'd she have explained that to the marshal?"

"What you aiming to do with that body in the yard?" Mac wanted to know.

"Eph doesn't know we're here," the Fiddler said. "He hasn't seen any of us, only heard someone creeping up on him. He doesn't know who but he does know two men were at the Diamond C. I'm going to try to think of some way to discredit him or put him in a position so he can't go to the law. He's bound, gagged, and blindfolded. I don't want him to have any idea where he is when he regains consciousness. We're going to take him deep into that stand of pine off the trail, hogtie his arms to his feet, and loop the rope around a tree so he can't even roll very far."

"Just leave him out there, Frank?" the Preacher asked.

"No," the Fiddler said. "I want a guard on him every minute. Work in pairs. If it's one man alone, he might fall asleep or take a notion to kill Eph. I don't want murder on my hands if it can be helped. Preacher, you and the Kid take the first watch, from now until dawn. Jake and Mac can relieve you. If you want to talk, get out of his hearing. Now let's get moving. Jake and Mac, get the mustangs and the roan. Preacher, you and the Kid lug out the saddles. Mac, you'll take Eph's horse and throw Eph over its neck. Jake will stay here with Boots until Mac and I come back. Preacher, take along anything you like except whiskey and don't let the Kid out of your sight."

The Fiddler was angry and tired and breathing hard when he finished. Jake and Mac went to the pasture and the Preacher and the Kid to the cave.

"Wouldn't it have been better to put him in the cave?" Boots asked when they were back in the kitchen.

"Only if we were sure we were going to kill him," he said as gently as he could. "Eph must never know about that cave."

"Frank?"

"Yes?"

"Is it going to be all right?" Her breast was fluttering and there were tears in her eyes but she wasn't crying.

He wrapped his arms around her and held her close. "Don't worry, Boots," he said softly. "I won't leave you to face this alone."

XIII

When the Fiddler left the Diamond C in the lilac-blue
dawn on Saturday morning, he rode Eph's black stud for a
very good reason. When Mac and he had returned from
the pine prison where Eph was secured with two guards,
the Fiddler had discovered that the horse wore no brand.

He was deeply concerned over the problems Eph raised.
There seemed no way short of murder to silence him and
although he had considered killing him as the final solution, he knew that when it came to the act he could never
do it, nor permit his death at any other's hand. It seemed
an insoluble situation and it cast a grim pall over the day.

He accompanied Jake and Mac into the thick timber. In
the cool, dark fastness of the small forest, they dismounted
some distance from the place he'd left Eph trussed up and
under guard. He wanted Eph to know as little of their
number and comings and goings as possible. Leaving Jake
and Mac with the horses, he walked without sound on the
needle-carpeted floor until he found the Preacher with his
back to a tree facing the captive. The Preacher's face was
haggard but he was awake. Eph was motionless in his
bonds and may have been sleeping. The Kid was stretched
out full length and snoring.

"Psst," the Fiddler hissed softly.

The Preacher's head jerked around and he smiled faintly
when he saw the Fiddler, who beckoned him.

When they were beyond hearing, the Fiddler asked, "Any trouble?"

"Oh no," the Preacher said indecisively. "I'll be glad to roll in."

"The Kid didn't spell you?"

The Preacher shrugged.

"Go get the Kid," the Fiddler told Mac when they reached him and Jake. "You know where we left Eph." To the Preacher, he said, "Take both horses. When you've turned them out, sleep easy until I get back. The Kid's staying out here."

The Preacher chuckled. "I knew I could depend on you, Frank." His expression quickly turned serious. "What are we going to do with him?"

"It's gnawing at my brains," the Fiddler said. "I'll get the horses and we'll go ahead as we planned. We're riding tonight. We can't leave him. We can't take him with us."

The three of them looked mutely at each other.

Mac brought the Kid, and Jake went to the prisoner. The Preacher mounted one of the mustangs, and the Kid started for the other.

"No, Kid." The Fiddler caught him by the belt and spun him around. "You're staying here with Jake and Mac."

"What makes you think that, friend?" the Kid asked, softly menacing.

"We're not taking chances with you today," the Fiddler said quietly. "You've got calves' jelly for brains. Mac, if he gives you any trouble, put him to sleep."

"You got no right to order me around, friend," the Kid snarled to the Fiddler.

"You heard what he said," Mac said good-naturedly, cuffing him with a bear swipe that toppled him.

The Preacher rode off with both horses, laughing quietly.

"If he kicks over the traces, I'll knock his jaw back so far he can scratch the back of his neck with his front teeth," Mac said pleasantly as he lifted the Kid's knife and gun.

Although the moon had been full when the band had come over the trail three nights before, it had been difficult to properly assess it. Now in the light of day the Fiddler found it well screened from view by juniper, piñon, and scrub pine. At places the brush thinned and the trace dipped into gulches and ravines. At the sides of some of these gulleys he saw tunnels and the timbers of shafts where the hills had been prospected. In one sheltered draw, he tied the black to a scrub oak and clawed his way through the prickly brush to an abandoned shaft almost completely concealed by the growth. Standing on the uphill side, he could look over the top of the shoring. The depths lay in blackness. He kicked a stone the size of a cabbage loose from the clay and dropped it into the pit. Several moments passed before he heard it thud on the bottom.

He was soberly thoughtful when he picked up the reins again. The trail was used little, the shaft concealed and deep. If it became necessary to dispose of Eph's body, it would be a good place. Although Eph was a murderer, such reflections distressed him. He could not avoid them. He was faced with bitter reality. The band could survive. Boots could not.

Carson City was no great distance, only eighteen miles or so from the Diamond C, and the black had a good lope when the high trail permitted. It was about seven o'clock when he sloped into an alley, an interim hour between the time men went to work in the mines and on the range and when the stores and offices opened. Few were on the main street and only the saloons and restaurants showed any activity.

Carson City was like Virginia City except, being the state capital, more substantial, with many buildings of sandstone. He met no riders on the hard-packed dirt street but when he found the assayer's frame building, the rack in front of the Golden Nugget saloon across the road was nearly full. He wanted the anonymity of the saloon rail and hitched the black at the end of the lineup.

The black was a splendid animal with a star between its eyes and four white stockings. The stud stood a good fifteen hands and had a steady gait. He wondered that Eph had not branded him. As he stood, he was anyone's mount.

A mercantile emporium and an apothecary shop down the boardwalk from the saloon was the Great West Cafe. It was well patronized with men who looked like a cross section of the town's population, miners or prospectors in rough clothes, businessmen in suit coats, merchants in vests, a lawyer, a doctor, a banker, perhaps, some drummers. He ordered a stack of sourdough cakes with two eggs and a steak and when he was finished had two cups of coffee and three cigarettes. It was eight o'clock when he opened the door to the assayer's office. It was a small one-room place with a counter and an enormous black safe.

The assayer was just getting out his avoirdupois scales. He was a mild-appearing, smooth-cheeked man in his forties with rimless half glasses and intelligent gray eyes. "Sir?" he inquired after swiftly appraising the Fiddler with a glance that seemed approving.

The Fiddler tossed the tobacco pouch on the unvarnished pine counter. "Would you evaluate this?"

The assayer pulled the thongs apart, seemed surprised at what he saw, and emptied the gold shavings on a china platter. He took the platter to a bench where he opened some blue bottles and performed some tests and then carefully transferred the shavings to a scoop. He placed this on a scale and fiddled with weights until it was in balance and announced to the Fiddler, "Twelve hundred and fifty dollars, give or take a few pennies."

It was difficult but the Fiddler kept a straight face. The sum was far more than he'd expected. There was ten times the weight of the pouch in the buckskin bag at the quartz cave, and the face of the vein had scarcely been scratched. "This is my first venture," he said. "What is the procedure? Will the bank give me credit on an account or cash for this gold?"

"Yes," the assayer said as he lighted a straight briar pipe while he retreated behind it in thought. After a few moments, he puffed decisively. "You're well bred and forthright. You say you're new to this field and a man would be a fool not to believe you. I'm going to give you a word of advice: What you've found is apparent from what you have here. If you take this gold to the bank word will race through town and your life won't be worth living. I'm the official assayer and I buy for the government. I can give you a voucher, which you can take to the bank, and they'll give you cash or a bank draft or open an account."

"Your advice is more priceless than the gold," the Fiddler said. "I'll take the voucher. The name is Franklyn Bye. What is your preference in whiskey?"

The assayer smiled slightly. "That is not necessary . . . although I do enjoy a sip of Old Crow before supper." He made out the voucher.

At the Great Western Bank he accepted their draft for one thousand dollars payable to Boothe Carrington and took two hundred and fifty dollars in gold coin, which he placed in the tobacco pouch. His feelings were mixed as he started for the Golden Nugget saloon to buy the whiskey for the assayer. He was happy for Boots and the one-thousand-dollar bank draft but uncertain about himself and the twelve thousand, five hundred dollars' worth of gold still in the cave. And there was Eph.

A very large red-faced man wearing a star on his vest was paying far too much attention to the black horse, studying his cannons and muzzle and looking for the brand. The Fiddler walked on without showing interest, turned at the corner, and located the back entrance to the saloon by the beer kegs stacked in the alley. There was a short hallway between storerooms and he stayed back in the shadows. He could see eight or ten men lined up at the bar.

The batwings flew back and the sheriff burst in as the Fiddler had expected he would. At the taps near the middle of the bar, the sheriff leaned over for confidential words with the bardog. "Ferd, who belongs to the black at the rail?" his voice boomed.

"What black?" Ferd asked indifferently and drew a stein.

"You didn't see him tie up? Nobody come in?" the sheriff asked militantly.

"They been coming and going all morning," Ferd said. "I didn't see nobody tie up. I ain't got time to watch the rack."

"Any strangers been in?"

"Hell yes, there been strangers, Gus," the bartender said impatiently. "Half the people in town always is strangers." He moved away with the stein.

"Any you boys see who tied up that black?" the sheriff addressed the bar.

No one responded, but one cowpoke went to the batwings to look out.

"That's the black was stole off George Merrill last
week," the sheriff announced. "George never bothered
branding him because he didn't like burning that beauty's
hide. Figured with the size and star on its nose and white
nobody'd dast take him for being recognized. I'm going to
keep my eye on that horse if it takes me all day. When that
varmint that stole him has had enough snake water to see
double, he'll come reeling back for the black and we'll have
us a horsethief."

He slapped the batwings and bellied out.

Unseen and unheard, the Fiddler left the way he'd
come, out the back door and into the alley, where the sun
baked the stink solid. Eph was capable of stealing the
black. Eli had accused him of starting his herd by rustling.
But the Fiddler did not think Eph had hustled the horse.
He was too shrewd for such open-handed thievery. The
Fiddler thought it more likely Eph had been trapped by his
greed and bested by the horsethief. Offered a fine animal at
a calamity price, Eph would find the bargain hard to resist,
especially since an unbranded horse belonged to the man
who rode it—except this distinctively marked black in this
one particular town.

At the far end of the alley, the Fiddler slipped incon-
spicuously into the crowd that was filling the boardwalk.
Stores and offices were opening and men were intent on
the start of the day's labors. At the Silver Dollar saloon he
hoisted one for himself, bought a quart for the Preacher
and himself on the road, and ordered a half barrel of Old
Crow delivered to the office of the government assayer.

The livery stable owner was a sour-faced old man without any teeth. His pointed nose seemed to touch his chin

when he talked. He was of the opinion that the purchase
of five riding horses and one saddle involved a morning of
bargaining and took a fresh chew of tobacco to prepare
himself for the haggling. When the Fiddler didn't dicker
because time was more important than ten or twenty dollars, the crotchety codger became downright genial, broke
out a jug of redeye, and filled two cups. There was some
horseshoeing to be done but he put the string together in a
hurry: a sturdy claybank with a comfortable Cheyenne saddle and four sound mustangs. The claybank carried a Hobbled O brand and the mustangs all wore Crazy 3s. The
Fiddler remembered to get legal, individual bills of sale on
the horses. The transaction had been swift. There were
times, the Fiddler reflected, when a black broadcloth frock
coat and a poke filled with gold were conveniences. He'd
paid two hundred dollars for the outfit and after breakfast,
a drink, and the bottle, there still remained forty-seven dollars from the two-fifty the Preacher had given him. Boots,
as was right, had paid for the assayer's half barrel.

It was a little after nine o'clock when he started for the
high trail. The narrow alley that led to it was lined with
cribs and tumbledown shacks. It was fouled with offal and
filled with flies that set the horses' tails switching. Although the hillside where the town ended was barren and
burned, the hot air was clean. The morning was brittle
bright and going to be another sizzler. He took off his collar and tie and opened the neckband. When he unbuttoned
the frock coat, the .44 was at his hand if he needed to use
it.

That thought put a smile to his lips. He slapped leather
a few times and was a fast draw but he'd never had to
shoot at a man. Something always had happened, like with
the Kid. He undoubtedly would have killed the Kid if the

Preacher hadn't slapped the gun from his hand. The way things had turned out, it was too bad the Preacher had interfered. They'd have been better off with the Kid dead. For a man who was ready to hang up his gunbelt, his attitude was strange. The night before, in the grip of outrage, he'd been ready to gun down Eph. He didn't like to think about it.

It was a miserable, plodding ride through the brush. The crumbling, dry growth and dust from the trail settled in his nostrils and throat and he had no canteen. The whiskey he'd drunk popped out in sweat. He had to hold the gait to a walk to keep the mustangs in line. At any other pace they'd have bolted.

He judged it must be nearing noon when he reached the heavy stand of pine. Jake and Mac had the Kid between them. They were sitting within sight but out of Eph's hearing. The captive was threshing and making gurgling sounds in his throat.

The Kid was a bundle of fury. "You're holding me prisoner like him, friend," he accused shrilly.

"Maybe you'd like the same treatment he's going to get," the Fiddler suggested with contempt in his voice. "You tried to kill me. That's what got us into this."

The Kid glowered and swore but he quieted.

Jake and Mac got up to inspect the mustangs. "Looks like they'll do," Jake observed.

"One had a loose shoe," the Fiddler said, still sitting the claybank. "The stable fixed it. I've got the bills of sale. We're ready to ride out tonight."

"I'm itching to go," Mac said. "For a safe hideout, this place has been busy as a saloon on Saturday night."

"We'll travel soon as it's dark," the Fiddler said. "Kid, get over there and hobble the mustangs."

The Kid took his time getting to his feet and he gave the Fiddler a dark look before he went to the horses.

Jake curled the ends of his mustache and glanced glumly in the direction of Eph. "What about him?"

That was the bitter decision the Fiddler had to make. "We can't take him with us and we can't leave him here. It's something that will have to be settled soon. Have any trouble with him?"

Mac's laughter rumbled. "He ain't in what you'd call high spirits."

Whatever the Fiddler decided to do about Eph, he'd have to live with it and he might find it intolerable. So far he'd been able to think of only one answer. "I'll send the Preacher out so you two can come in."

"Hey, friend, how about me?" the Kid demanded.

"You stay put, boy, until we're ready to ride," the Fiddler said coldly.

The Kid changed his tactics. "I'm hungry and I'm thirsty," he whined.

"I'll have the Preacher bring out some biscuits and water," the Fiddler said.

"Biscuits and water!" the Kid howled. "I need coffee and food. Hear me, friend? And I need my knife. I got to cut this line for rope to hobble the mustangs."

"Cut it for him where he wants, Mac," the Fiddler said. He reined the claybank about. "Don't let him get his hands on that blade. He'd slit your throat. The Preacher should be here in a half hour or so."

The Fiddler gave the horse a drink at the trough and put him out of sight in the stall next to the cow and the calf. Boots was not in the garden so he went to the house. Heidi bounded from the kitchen to meet him, and Boots came to the door. She was wearing Levi's and an oversized shirt.

There was no smile on her lips and her eyes were solemn.

"Is everything all right, Frank?" she asked anxiously.

"Everything is all right," he assured her. He did not like the role he was forced to play, telling her one thing when he knew in his mind the fact was quite different.

"Eph?"

"Still with us, alive and kicking. Don't worry about him. He isn't going to bother you again."

"You're going to kill him," she whispered, and her face grew pale.

He could not give her that knowledge. It would haunt her nights the rest of her life. "He will come to no harm by my hand," he promised.

"You'll order one of the others to do it," she said wretchedly.

"I would never do that," he said firmly. "Forget Eph. He is no longer a problem."

"But how?" she faltered.

"There are matters in Eph's past he would not want revealed," he said, wishing he had proof Eph had murdered Eli. It was a thought and worth a try. "He can be convinced. You might call it blackmail. Under the circumstances, I'd call it a swap. He won't talk."

"Oh Frank, I'm so relieved," she said and caught her breath. "I'm sorry. I've been thoughtless. I was so worried. Have dinner with me."

"A glass of water," he said and smiled stiffly. He'd committed himself with his assurance Eph would not talk. Actually, nothing had changed. He'd just been putting off the final decision until now. "A cup of coffee. I had dinner for breakfast this morning."

He glanced about the kitchen. Anything to get his mind

onto something else. It was a good kitchen. He'd paid little attention to it before. The house was small but the kitchen was large, a living room-kitchen. He wondered why Eli hadn't built a fireplace. There was room for one. With a big fireplace, it would be a cozy room. Even without a fireplace, it was comfortable and homey. A square table with two chairs in the middle of the room was covered with a blue and white checkered cloth. Four chairs were placed about the table. A large black range occupied the bedroom wall, placed there no doubt to provide heat for both rooms. There were three windows with white curtains, two opening onto the porch and the third looking out on the garden. It was over a zinc basin with a hand pump. There was a large, curtained pine cupboard, a horsehair sofa, and a matching armchair.

"How was the garden this morning?" he asked. One place was set at the table and he took the chair opposite it.

"Oh wonderfully moist," she said happily. He'd banished her fears and now she could turn her mind to the sunny side of the day. "I let the gate down and it shut off the flow. It works just like you said it would." She brought him a cup of coffee. "Are you sure you won't eat? It isn't much, it's so warm. Just a salad from the garden and some cheese."

He shook his head. "Thanks, no, Boots. I have to talk to the Preacher and send him out to relieve Jake and Mac."

"Then I'll just have coffee with you," she said with a warm smile. She poured a cup and sat across from him. "I'm so pleased you worked it out about Eph. What's a little blackmail? Poof! Did you get your horses?"

"Yes." She hadn't once mentioned the mortgage. "They're hidden in the woods."

"You'd think of that," she said, half-teasing. "You always think of everything."

"If only I could," he said. "You ride, of course."

"Of course," she said lightly. "And not sidesaddle."

"Will you go to town this afternoon? And not take the wagon. The team is too slow."

"Certainly, Frank." She seemed pleased that he'd ask. "What is it you need? I don't have any good riding clothes, like some of the rich ladies. Only Levi's and shirts like this. But it doesn't matter."

If only she knew, he thought, and agreed, "No, how you dress doesn't matter, especially today. When you have money in your pocket, you can have holes in your socks. You have a legacy from Eli." He laid the bank check for one thousand dollars before her. She picked it up and stared at it, read the figures, and reread them. Her lips parted and for a moment she did not breathe. When she looked at him, her eyes lacked comprehension.

"What does this mean?" she asked.

Despite the distasteful day that lay ahead, he chuckled. "I didn't hold up the bank. They don't write drafts for thieves. I didn't buy it with stolen money. We don't have that much, anyway. None of it came from any private funds of my own. I have none." He dropped the tobacco pouch in front of her. It clinked. She opened it and spilled the gold coins on the table. She did not speak. He did not think she could even see. Her dark eyes brimmed with tears.

"There's two hundred dollars," he said. "It was two hundred and fifty but there were expenses that I felt well met. Pay off the mortgage and open a savings account. Buy something foolish you don't need."

She found her tongue at last. "I don't understand. You said a legacy from Eli. The most money he ever had at one time was when he mortgaged the property. Whatever you say, this must be something you've managed to do."

"No, Boots," he said quietly. "The money comes from something of Eli's I found in the cave. Take it in good faith. It is legally and rightfully yours."

"What could he possibly have possessed that would be of such value?"

"No more questions." He pushed back his chair and stood. "Perhaps someday I'll tell you. I'm sorry but I have to see the Preacher."

She flew from her chair and threw her arms around him, laying her head against his chest. "I can't—" She began to sob.

"Then don't." He kissed her gently. A tear tumbled from her nose onto his cheek.

She stepped away, blinking. "What shall I say when they ask? They'd never believe Eli left such a sum to me."

"They won't argue with money," he said wryly, "but you're right about Eli. Don't mention him at all. Say that it came from a friend back home. A very dear friend."

That had been part of his original plan, the mortgage money from the very dear friend back home. Then the arrival of the friend. It wouldn't make any difference to him now. When he'd done what had to be done about Eph, he'd have to put her out of his life but the story still would serve her and conceal the actual source of the funds.

"You're riding tonight," she said, stepping onto the porch with him.

"Yes."

"I'll hurry back from town." The dancing lights were back in her eyes. "There are things to talk about now that the place is clear and there's money to start irrigating the entire bench. We have so much planning to do."

XIV

There was no joy left in the Fiddler when he started for the barn. He was suffering and made no effort to hide it from himself. He'd carry the deception through this day and she'd not know for a while. Gradually, as the weeks and months marched on and there was no word from him, she'd come to accept the fact that he wasn't coming back. It would hurt but it would be a slow, dull pain that finally would diminish. Her nights would be bad but she'd have her work to occupy her days. She'd irrigate the bench, now that she knew how, and prosper in worldly goods if not in her heart. He ached with thought of what might have been. He'd come to the fork in the trail and he'd thought he'd known which path he'd take. All that was changed. With Eph's murder, although he was never caught, he'd be forever outside the law in his own mind. Things could have been different.

He lifted the quart of whiskey from the saddlebag and took it into the cave. The Preacher was at the table finishing his breakfast. He looked startled when the Fiddler poured a cup of whiskey for himself and pushed the bottle to him.

"What's wrong, Frank?" he asked, alarmed.

"Nothing," the Fiddler said dully. "I brought back the horses. We'll ride out tonight as we planned and we'll be in Cheyenne within a week."

"You're in the doldrums," the Preacher said. He did not reach for the bottle. "What is it?"

"I'm going to kill Eph," the Fiddler said.

"I'll do it," the Preacher said quietly.

The Fiddler shook his head. "It would be the same thing. As long as it must be done, let me do it and have one guilt instead of two."

The Preacher poured some whiskey in a cup for himself. "I understand. I'm sorry." He took a long drink. "When?"

"About sundown, shortly before we leave, when normal people are off the trails and roads." The Fiddler set his jaw. "I've found a safe place to dispose of the body. I doubt they'll ever find it." He emptied his cup. "I'll bring in the mustang and the roan and help you saddle them. Boots is riding the other mustang to town. There's a claybank in a stall. It's one of the horses I bought. I may want to use it. The others are mustangs. They're in the trees. Take water and biscuits to the Kid. I'm keeping him off the place until we're ready to leave."

He carried one of Boots' saddles to the corral and left it on the rail and went to the pasture for the two mustangs and the roan. When he returned for Boots' second saddle, the Preacher was putting a can of beans and cold bacon with the biscuits in the saddlebag. "I'd forgotten we'll be taking one of Boots' saddles," the Fiddler said and tossed his poke to the Preacher. "There's forty-seven dollars left. Better pay her."

He carted the second saddle into the barn, and the Preacher lugged the one for the roan. Heidi romped up to welcome the Preacher.

"Get back inside," the Preacher told the Fiddler. "Have another drink. Lie down for a while and get some rest. You'll need it tonight. I'll saddle up."

"Thanks, Preacher," the Fiddler said. "I'll do that before I start putting our things together."

He built a cigarette, had a swallow from the bottle, and took a lantern to the small tunnel that led to the quartz cave. He could not say exactly what was in his mind. When he'd shucked his gunbelt, shed his shirt, and pulled off his boots, he wormed his way under the slab of granite and walked into the dazzle of the treasure cave. He looked about with aversion, seeing no beauty in the bubbling spring with the vein of gold above nor in the creamy white walls that reflected the light in faceted sparkles. Curious in a detached sort of way, he hefted the bucksin bag. It was a good ten times heavier than the tobacco pouch had been, perhaps much more. A considerable wealth. Idly, he picked up the chisel and pressured it with the palm of his left hand across the vein of gold. Even without the mallet, he scraped off a shaving of gold. He considered it a moment and threw it to the floor.

He was of the pack now, one of them. He'd hunt with them and kill with them and share the spoils. Their life would be his life and he'd come to the same end. It wouldn't be the way it had been before. The game was over. It would be a deadly business from now on.

"Boots wouldn't take the money, Frank. She said she didn't need it."

The Fiddler turned slowly and faced the Preacher. The Fiddler was not surprised. In the back of his mind he'd known all along that the Preacher was aware of the quartz cave. The Preacher had removed his gunbelt but his .44 dangled in his hand at his side. There was no expression on his face but his eyes were glowing strangely. The Fiddler looked at him calmly and did not speak.

"I believed you, Frank, when you said you hadn't come

through." The Preacher was not reproachful. There was no tone to his voice. Like his face, it was expressionless. "I wanted to believe you. I didn't want you to know about the gold."

The Fiddler said unemotionally, "It was you who killed Eli. How did you know his secret?"

The Preacher's voice made his words a litany. "He spent too much time in the barn. I hid in the mow and saw him lift the feedbox and go into the tunnel. When he left, I investigated. There was nothing in the cavern that could account for the amount of time he spent inside so I explored the small tunnel and came upon this."

"And you killed your niece's husband for his gold." He knew the Preacher was going to kill him but the knowledge did not agitate him. It was as if this were the inevitable final act of a drama he was witnessing but in which he was not participating.

"Not for his gold," the Preacher said in monotone. "Because of it. Does Boots know?"

"I told her only that I'd found something in the cave that had belonged to Eli and the money was her legacy." He should be thinking of some action he could take but he felt no inclination to move. "I told her nothing of the gold."

"I'd hoped as much, Frank, and of course, you wouldn't." The Preacher's eyes were the eyes of a zealot. "I'm happy your greed kept you from telling her. It would agonize me to have to kill her too."

It was an academic question but the Fiddler felt he had to ask. "Since you killed Eli for the gold, why haven't you taken it?" The Fiddler had not moved since he'd turned to the Preacher.

"You misunderstood, Frank," the Preacher chanted. "I

said *because of* it, not *for* it. Gold is evil. It fills man with avarice and malice. It despoils him and fills him with lust and hate. It reduces him to a beast. I killed Eli to keep him from his gold so he could not destroy Boots."

Some faint feeling stirred the Fiddler. "Preacher," he said with a smile, "you've spent your life stealing from others. How do you reconcile what you say with what you've done?"

"I took what they had to save them from themselves," the Preacher said as if by rote. "I already was fated to destruction but my doom was their salvation. I was the instrument. What I took from them was money. What I gave was hope."

"It's of small concern," the Fiddler said, "but I'm beginning to understand you. You've never really tried to save anyone. You've been trying to vindicate yourself. Since that congregation put you down because of your appearance, you've turned your spite on all mankind."

The Preacher ignored the comment or did not hear. "I'm truly sorry, Frank. Of all the men I've known, you alone did not seem to covet possessions. Now that you have been touched and are one of them, I shall have to kill you."

A moving shadow in the tunnel passed the Fiddler's eyes. It alerted him and restored his normal reactions. "Quick, Preacher," he warned sharply, "there's someone behind you in the tunnel."

"That ploy is unworthy of you," the Preacher said without feeling.

The Kid rammed his .44 into the Preacher's back. "Drop your gun, old man."

The Preacher's eyes went dull. His face sagged and he did as he was told.

The Kid stepped into the cave and kicked the gun back to the tunnel. His dark eyes darted from Preacher to Fiddler, to the vein in the wall and the bag on the floor. He sidled around the wall, tense, gun ready to fire. When he reached the bag, he pulled it back along the wall with him and opened it, not looking inside but reaching for a handful of gold. When he saw what he held, he laughed shrilly. He dropped the shavings back into the bag. "Ho friends, a secret this big you should have shared. Now I have to kill you both."

"You see, Frank, gold is evil and fills man with lust," the Preacher intoned.

The Kid was standing against the wall and between the Preacher and the Fiddler. "I think first the old man so the Fiddler can see what is coming to him and suffer a little," he said with apparent great satisfaction.

The Fiddler still held the chisel in his right hand. He'd gradually let it slide down until it rested in his palm, blade at his fingertips. When the Kid turned his gun to the Preacher, the Fiddler hurled the chisel in a mighty underhand cast. The pitch was hurried and higher than the mark he had set. The blade struck the Kid at the base of the throat and imbedded itself almost to the haft. The Fiddler did not know whether the Kid had fired before the chisel struck him or whether a reflex had pulled the trigger. The Kid was dead on the floor. The Preacher had crashed backward into the tunnel and was not breathing. The stain on his shirt was above his heart.

The Fiddler pulled the chisel from the Kid's throat and bound the gash with his shirt to stanch the blood. He dragged the body through the tunnel to the granite shaft and left it with arms over head so he could reach the hands. He crawled over the dead man and, feet first under the slab, took hold of the hands, and worked the corpse into the cave. He returned for the Preacher's body and a third time for the lantern and bag of gold. The chisel and mallet and blood stains were left behind.

He worked swiftly without feeling, bundling the bodies in red blankets and roping the flaps over the heads and the feet. He'd removed all property from each, the Kid's gunbelt and knife, the Preacher's poke and a cache of twenty double eagles sewn in the Preacher's waistband. He put them with the two hundred and fifty dollars the Preacher had in his poke and the forty-seven dollars he'd given him. When he was done with the shrouds, he put on his boots, shirt, hat, and gunbelt but he did not bother with collar or frock coat. When he'd buckled the bag of gold shavings in the claybank's saddlebag, he climbed onto the Preacher's roan and started for the embankment leading the mustang. He did not even take time to hobble the horse the Kid had ridden bareback from the trees.

"The Kid—" Jake started to say when the Fiddler reached Mac and him.

"Never mind," the Fiddler said. "We're leaving right now. Stay with Eph. Mac and I will take the string in, pack up, and bring your horse to you."

Mac and Jake unhobbled the three mustangs and they drove them over the trail and up the embankment. They put them in the corral with the fourth Crazy 3 horse. The Fiddler had remained silent and Mac hadn't asked questions.

"Pick out the two best," the Fiddler now said. "Turn the others to pasture along with the roan and the Diamond C mustang. Hang these saddles in the barn. I'll bring out the new ones. I have a Cheyenne for the claybank."

There were large questions in Mac's eyes but he went to

work without a word. Again, the Fiddler did not feel a part of what he was doing. Without being told, Mac brought the two Crazy 3 horses he'd selected into the barn when the Fiddler carried out the second saddle and all the red blankets.

"When the mustangs are saddled come into the cave," he told Mac.

Mac nodded his shaggy head, puzzled but following orders.

The Fiddler was separating what they'd need and could carry when Mac clomped to the table.

"Where's the Preacher and the Kid?" he finally asked, unable to wait any longer for answers.

The Fiddler handed the bottle of the whiskey to him and pointed to the blanketed shapes by the stream. "The Kid shot the Preacher. I stabbed the Kid." He'd never know whether the Kid shot before he died and he didn't see what difference it made. "We'll have to get rid of the bodies."

Mac whistled, took a long drink, and didn't ask any more questions.

When everything they could carry was in the saddlebags and in the blanket rolls behind the cantles, Mac and the Fiddler each swung a corpse over his shoulder and tied the bodies in front of the saddlehorns over the shoulders of the mustangs. The Fiddler returned to the cave for the last time. There was some blood by the stream where the bodies had lain and he scrubbed it away with a towel. Everything else seemed in order. Pots, pans, things they didn't need were rinsed and stacked on the table. The cartridge cases were upright and in place. The fat lamps were extinguished. He fastened on his collar and string tie, thrust into the frock coat, and took a bulky flour sack and the lanterns with him. He left his old clothing and the fiddle and bow behind.

The Fiddler hung the lanterns in the barn and carried the flour sack to the kitchen. Mac had the horses waiting in the yard. The Fiddler dumped the flour sack by the cupboard and placed the sugar bowl over the bills of sale for the Crazy 3 mustangs. He did not write a note.

With the Preacher's and the Kid's gunbelts slung over the horn of the claybank's saddle, the Fiddler led the cortege to the embankment. Heidi ran along to the edge of the bench, barked twice, and turned back to the house. The Fiddler did not turn his head.

Jake took the news stolidly but did have a question. "What about him?" he asked, indicating Eph.

The Fiddler unhooked the two gunbelts from the horn of his saddle and gave one to each of them. "Wear them," he said. "We'll put Eph in front of my saddle. Tie his hands and feet together under the horse and throw a hitch over the horn."

They rode single file in silence, the Fiddler taking the lead. When they neared the abandoned shaft he'd explored, he pulled up. They hitched the horses to scrub pine, and Jake and Mac carried the bodies through the brush. The Fiddler toted the Bourbon.

"Ain't there something to say?" Mac asked gruffly.

There wasn't much compassion left in the Fiddler. He looked at the remains of the Preacher and the Kid perched on the shoring, ready to plunge into eternity, and removed his hat. Jake and Mac did the same. "*Vaya con Dios*," the Fiddler said.

When the two bundles thumped far below in the pit, the Fiddler uncorked the bottle and gave it to Jake. He passed it to Mac. The Fiddler finished what was left and pitched the bottle after the bodies. The final tribute.

"Does he go next?" Jake asked, jerking his head toward the trail.

"Not yet," the Fiddler said.

They rode on without speaking in the airless ovenheat of the midafternoon. Now and then Eph grunted and struggled. He was still alive. Just before they reached the hill above Carson City where the trail dipped to the squalid alley, the Fiddler reined in. He dismounted and drew Jake and Mac well away from the horses into the piñon and divided the coin from the Preacher's poke. Two hundred dollars each for Jake and for Mac, one hundred ninety-seven for himself. He gave each the bill of sale for his horse.

"You ain't coming with us," Mac said, eyes saddening. "This has been one hell of a day."

"All the provisions, the pots and pans, everything you'll need is in your saddlebags and rolls," he told them. "You have enough in your pokes to keep out of trouble. I'm going to take one last gamble. If it works, I'll go my way. If it doesn't, no need for you to hang with me. The Preacher said this trail is an owlhoot and skirts the town to the west through the hills. Keep to it and you'll be in California by morning. We've never ridden in California so you should be safe there until you pull your first raid."

"You gambling on him?" Jake asked in astonishment.

The Fiddler nodded his head. "I've killed one man today, but that was different. Killing Eph would be cold-blooded murder. Maybe he'll cross up himself. It's a chance I've got to take."

Mac was perspiring freely. He pulled off his hat and shook himself like a big shaggy dog. "I ain't much for saying things but it was good, riding with you. There was always something to laugh at. If you should live, maybe our trails will cross."

"Damn fool idea you're following," Jake said morosely, "but I give you my best."

The Fiddler nodded his head soberly. "One more thing: I think Eph's conscious. He was twitching and groaning back there. I don't want him to hear my voice. Jake, go tell him his horse is hitched at the Golden Nugget saloon."

XV

The Fiddler watched until Jake and Mac blended into the landscape. One way or another, for good or for bad, they were out of his life. There was neither regret nor relief at their departure. Whatever lay ahead for him, all the band was gone now, even the Fiddler. He was Franklyn Bye again, although he didn't look nor feel like the young man he'd been.

Eph was making brutish noises in his throat and trying to kick. It was spooking the claybank. Frank tapped Eph on the back of his head with the butt of his gun and he went limp.

Still screened from the town but near the beginning of the alley, Frank pushed a few yards to a clump of juniper bushes off the trail. He freed Eph from the claybank's neck, stretched him out on the ground, and cut the bonds on his wrists. He did not untie his ankles. He'd brought Eph's hat, boots, and guns in a saddlebag and he laid them where Eph would see them when he ripped off the blindfold. Then he went through Eph's pockets to make certain the Kid had not pilfered his poke. It was intact, more than six hundred dollars.

Although it was only a little after four o'clock, the town was beginning to feel like Saturday night, and the hitchrails at the saloons were filled. The bank was open until five o'clock, he noted, and tied up in front of the assay office. Without looking directly, he saw that the black with white stockings was still at the rack.

When he took the heavy bag into the assayer's office, the mild-mannered man greeted him cordially. "Your thoughtfulness overwhelmed me, Mr. Bye," he said. "I got the buggy and took the barrel home at dinnertime or I'd offer you a glass."

"And I'd have to decline," Frank said with a half smile. He lifted the bag onto the counter.

The assayer observed the weight and drew the front curtain. Then he came around the counter and locked the front door. At his bench, he worked silently with his tests and measures and when he was finished, said respectfully, "Seventeen thousand, eight hundred and fifty dollars." A faint smile lifted his pale lips and he added, "Give or take a dollar or two. You'll want a voucher, of course."

"Yes, a voucher, of course," Frank said.

This time he had the bank make out the draft for the full amount in the name of Franklyn Bye.

There were several things he wanted to do and he was in no hurry. It would take an hour at least before he learned whether his gamble paid off. He went into three stores before he found a suit that struck his fancy, the frock coat dove gray with satin lapels. They'd have the trousers hemmed and the waist taken in by five o'clock at the latest. There was a new pair of black boots with pointed toes, gentlemen's boots only eight inches high. A broad-brimmed, flat-crowned hat to match the suit, a white shirt with a soft collar and frilled front. A blue cravat and a pair of gray doeskin riding gloves. Underwear, socks, and handkerchief. A new man from the skin out. Actually, he did not favor the attire he selected. It was a costume for the part he'd play, if he got to go on with the act.

He took the new underwear and socks from the emporium with him to the barber shop, where he soaked long in
a very hot water bath. He smoked three cigarettes before
he called for rinse water. He lingered another five or ten
minutes before he dressed and returned to the store for his
new clothes. He was prepared and could do nothing further. He'd carried everything as far as he could. From now
on, events were out of his hands.

When he'd changed clothes, he wrapped Eli's suit and
his gunbelt in his roll and tied it to the cantle. Then he
crossed to the Golden Nugget. The black was gone. He
went into the saloon to wait.

The Golden Nugget was a large place, smoky and
sweaty, noisy and jampacked. Every kind of man was there.
Rich man, poor man, beggar man, and, he conceded, thief.
In the area next to the long bar there were tables and a
piano. Several painted cats prowled the tables. He edged to
the bar between a puncher and a shopkeeper, to judge by
their clothes. He was in no mood to talk with anyone, especially a fancy woman in a saloon.

He attracted some attention. Of course he would. He
looked like a gambler, or a fop, or a very rich man. The
men looked at him but they didn't engage him in conversation. His eyes felt like blue ice and he didn't think they
encouraged idle remarks.

Perhaps half an hour passed before he received the word
he'd been awaiting. Two cowpokes, a long one and a short
one, flipped the batwings and clattered in, laughing. They
stood behind him and he could feel the hot breath of their
guffaws on his neck. The storekeeper left and the pokes
bellied in.

"Gus took the cuss that stole George Merrill's black,"
the short puncher who had horse teeth told the bartender

when he brought them a bottle and glasses. He heehawed before he poured.

"That's good," the barman said and scratched the back of his neck. "What's so funny about it you got to laugh before you drink?"

"What he said, that rustler," the long poke said and both of them howled.

The bardog ignored calls for service. He hunched over the bar and declared, "Well, tell me now, what did he say?"

The tall cowboy had a hound-dog face that looked as if it never smiled but it cracked into a broad grin now. He poured a drink to limber his tonsils. "Gus was waiting for him, had been all day. He nailed him when he unhitched the black. First off, that cuss claimed he owned George Merrill's horse. Said he bought him off a saddle tramp for ten dollars. Only he couldn't show no sale bill."

"It's not all that funny, the way you were laughing," the barman said.

"That's just the start," said horseface. "Gus hauled him and the horse to the jug and sent for George Merrill. Meanwhile, this cuss is raving about being bushwhacked and beat and blindfolded and gagged and hogtied and robbed." He began to chortle again. "Only he's wearing two guns and when Gus has him empty his poke there's more'n six hundred dollars in it."

"How drunk was he?" the bartender asked, beginning to smile.

"Hard to tell for the stink," the one who looked like a hound dog said and his eyes were far from melancholy.

The barman was chuckling. "It's getting pretty good. Is there more?"

"You betcha!" the tall one said and slapped the bar.

"He claimed he hadn't rid that black horse here. Said he was brung here tied to the neck of a horse."

The bartender was laughing heartily. "And?"

"And dumped at some alley and walked into town," the dog-faced one said. "Only he don't know who brung him or what he looked like. All he heard was a whisper in his ear telling him where his horse was at."

"How the hell can a man think up a story like that less'n he's drunk as a fiddler?" the bartender asked.

Frank lifted an eyebrow at the remark but generally he was satisfied with what he heard.

"That still ain't all or the best," the little poke said. "George Merrill come in and said, 'Why sure, that's old Stockings.' Then this horsethief said he was a law-abiding citizen and rancher from Virginia City, and Gus asked him his name."

"That did it," said the puncher whose face looked as if it should have been sad but wasn't today. "The cuss said he was Eph Carrington, and that blew the whistle."

"Seems Gus has been laying for this Carrington for rustling," said the short one. "Claimed he'd knowed who was running off the cows but never could catch him."

The tall one was beginning to laugh again. "Said now he had him red-handed, he'd see he rotted in jail if he wasn't strung up."

Frank left four bits for the bardog, pulled on his riding gloves, and walked over to the claybank. The gamble had paid off far better than he'd hoped. He was satisfied to this point but he didn't allow himself to think further. Other barriers remained. He took the road this time to Virginia City, not pushing the claybank in the late afternoon heat but holding him to an easy canter. It was an hour before sundown when he reined in and tied up at the jailhouse in Virginia City.

Marshal Cyrus Fargo stared moodily at him when he came in the door. The marshal seemed depressed. Deputy Bart Axelrod lifted his hat for a glimpse and shoved it back over his eyes.

"Marshal?" Frank inquired.

"Marshal Fargo," Cyrus acknowledged. "Can I do something?" He sounded too weary to care.

"Can you tell me how to find Mrs. Boothe Carrington?" Frank asked.

The front legs of the deputy's chair thudded to the floor, and Frank felt his eyes searching him.

The marshal examined Frank closely. "You're a stranger hereabouts. Mrs. Carrington is a widow and lives by herself. Who might you be and what is your business with her?"

"A commendable precaution, Marshal," Frank said approvingly. "I'm a friend from Illinois. A very old friend. The name is Franklyn Bye."

"You wouldn't be that dear old friend sent the widow the money to pay off the mortgage?" the deputy asked directly.

"Hmm," Frank said. "Could you tell me the way to the Diamond C?"

"Of course, Mr. Bye," the marshal said, genial enough for the glumness that seemed to possess him. "About six miles north on the stage road. A small white house up a slope to the west. You can't miss it. It's the first place you'll come to."

"Thank you kindly," Frank said and turned to leave.

"She expecting you?" the deputy asked.

"I can't say," Frank said.

"I think she is," the deputy said with a smirk. "She bought a big steak and sent the butcher's boy to the saloon for a bottle of whiskey. I know the widow don't drink."

"Perhaps," Frank said, "she is expecting some other guest."

When Franklyn Bye had ridden off on his claybank, Bart jumped from his chair and slapped his thigh. "I hope she lands him!" he exclaimed. "Bejesus, I hope she does. Sent her one thousand dollars and come all the way from the East. I hope that poor little lady gets him."

"He's a gentleman," the marshal observed.

"And well-fixed to boot," Bart said enthusiastically. "Bejesus, what a day for the widow."

"Did you notice, Bart?" Fargo asked.

"Did I notice what?" Bart asked peevishly. Cyrus had been vague and indefinite all day.

"He wasn't carrying any iron." Fargo looked baffled. "His coat was open and he wasn't wearing a gunbelt."

Bart chuckled. "I guess they're civilized back East. He's a pilgrim. He'll learn."

"Oh he won't stay," Fargo said. "He's just come out here to take her away."

"Then why'd he send her the money to pay off the mortgage?" Bart asked logically. "We got us a solid new citizen."

Fargo's eyes were distant. After a moment he asked, "Did he remind you of anyone?"

"Never set my eyes on him afore this day," Bart said positively. "Never seen anybody in my entire life looked a bit like him with that black hair and mustache and thick sideburns and fine features. Don't go telling me he reminds you of the Fiddler. That's the only name you been able to say for more'n three days."

"That's it!" the marshal exclaimed.

Bart groaned. "Not that Fiddler tune again, Cyrus."

"No, not the Fiddler, of course not, any fool could see that," Fargo said scornfully. "It was that actor last summer. It was what you said about fine features reminded me. It was that actor that was some kind of prince. Hamlet, I think his name was. The prince, not the actor."

"I sure hope she lands him," Bart said and tilted his chair back against the wall.

XVI

It was somewhat too warm but a whisper of a breeze had come up in the last hour and the sunset was glorious, all golden and blue. It was a tranquil time of day. Man was done with the day's labor and home and at peace. Frank should have been content. Eph Carrington had proved his own undoing. Whatever his fate, the penitentiary or the noose, he would no longer harass anyone. The Fiddler had departed forever along with his band, and the marshal had accepted Franklyn Bye. He should have felt repose. He did not. The harshest test of all was yet to come.

He sat the claybank a moment, looking up the long slope toward the small house. The blaze of the sun was in his eyes but he imagined Boots sitting in her rocking chair, watching the road, and seeing him start up. She would wonder who he was.

He walked the claybank to the bench and ground-reined him. No one had called a greeting. Not even Heidi had romped out to meet him. Boots was not on the porch nor in the kitchen. Fear gripped him and he ran to the garden. She was not watching her vegetables grow but he heard Heidi's woof and looked up the new canal to the gate. Heidi was bounding toward him. Boots saw him and started to run. He heard a little cry shudder from Boots' throat, a keening, half sob, half laugh. She was sobbing when she came into his arms.

Long moments passed while she clung to him and then she stepped back wiping the tears from her cheek with the back of her hand. He gave her his handkerchief and she dabbed at her eyes and sniffed.

"I'm afraid I'm not very brave." The gamin-eyed urchin was wistful.

"Shall we sit on the porch and talk?" he asked gently.

"What is there to say?" Her eyes still were misty but she was smiling. "You came back." She sniffed once more. "Oh very well. Of course there are questions. We may as well get it over with so we can forget everything that is past. Unsaddle your horse and put him to pasture."

He let the horse drink from the trough, hung the saddle on the rail, and put him in the corral. On the porch, he removed his hat, frock coat, and tie, and opened his shirt collar.

"You're not wearing a gunbelt." She radiated joy. "Let's sit on the edge of the porch where we won't be so far apart." She sat down and jumped up. "Oh wait. No, don't wait. Sit down. I'll be right back."

She ran into the kitchen and he sat beside his coat. In a moment she was back with a quart bottle of whiskey and a glass. "I thought we'd have supper together before you rode off, and you might like a drink."

"And you bought a large steak and I wasn't here," he finished.

She was surprised. "How did you know that?"

He laughed easily. It was good to be with her again. "It's the sort of thing you would do."

"Franklyn Bye, you know me too well." She was still standing. "Is that really your name?"

"Yes, Boots, it always has been and still is." He uncorked the bottle. "Bring a glass for yourself with a little water. You've had quite a day. You'll find a weak drink relaxing." Before the evening was over, she might need a strong drink for a stimulant, he thought.

"Yes, Frank, a frenzied day." She ran to the kitchen and ran back with a glass half filled with water. "It may make me silly. They say whiskey does. I've never drunk whiskey before."

He touched the water with just enough whiskey to color it. She sat close to him and thrust her arm through his.

"Do you mind if I smoke?" he asked, reaching to his coat for the makings.

"Let me build it for you," she said eagerly and he handed the tobacco and papers to her. She rolled the cigarette quite deftly, touched the paper with her tongue, twisted the ends, and placed it between his lips.

"Thank you, Boots," he said and lighted it. He wished she'd drink her whiskey. She was far too excited.

"Oh I forgot," she said abruptly. "I didn't tell you how elegant you look, Frank. And me still in my Levi's and shirt."

"I'd be more comfortable in my western outfit," he said. "These clothes were meant to impress Franklyn Bye on a person. That's all."

"And did they?"

"They did."

"You haven't poured your drink yet," she pointed out.

"So I haven't," he said absently. He poured two fingers in his glass. "Cheers," he said, toasting her.

"Is that how you do it? Don't you bump glasses? Cheers." She clinked her glass against his and took a long swallow.

"It isn't water, Boots," he said and laughed. "Sip it."

She made a face. "It tastes like medicine."

"Good medicine. You're jumpy."

"Yes, I'm jumpy, I'm twittery, I'm nerves all over. I didn't know what to think. I've been beside myself all afternoon. Too much has happened too fast. Why don't you start talking?"

"We left in a hurry," he began.

She couldn't wait. The questions she'd been asking herself all day tumbled out. "Yes, I know. Whatever happened? I was so worried. There was the sack of flour in the kitchen and sale bills for two mustangs. I found the horses in the pasture. That meant that two didn't go. Who didn't go, Frank? Where are they? I kept hoping maybe it was you and Milford who'd stayed. I rapped on the feedbox and rapped and rapped. I finally took a lantern and went into the cave and no one was there and everything was gone except two cups and plates and some pots and pans and your old clothes and your fiddle. Why did you leave your fiddle behind? I rode into the pines and found where the horses had been and where you'd tied Eph and no one was there, either. What did you do to Eph? Oh Frank, it's been a wretched day after starting so fine."

"Easy, Boots," he said and put his arm around her. "All that is what I'm trying to tell you."

She jumped to her feet. "Would you like supper now? I did buy a big steak."

"First we must talk."

"Yes, Frank." She sat beside him and sipped at her drink.

"I won't go into details," he said soberly. "I'll give you the bare facts. Some of them are brutal. I'm sorry but I think you should know. The Kid killed the Preacher. I killed the Kid."

"Oh how awful!" She buried her face in her hands.

He put his arm around her again and felt she was weeping quietly. It did not last long. She sat up and held her hand out for his handkerchief. "Keep it," he said.

"Will I need it again?"

"I don't think so, but keep it."

"Yes, Frank. I'm all right now."

"We did not harm Eph but he's in jail at Carson City and may hang. They arrested him for a horsethief. He didn't steal the horse but he must have known it had been stolen at the price he paid for it. They'd been trying to catch him rustling. The property is clear now. Whatever they do with him, he'll never bother you."

"I can guess how he got to Carson City," she said. "Did you know about the horse?"

"Yes. It was either that or murder him."

"I shed no tears for him," she said.

"Jake and Mac are on their way to California. They'll not ride this way again."

"I didn't mind them," she said with a whimsical smile. "I won't miss them but it did seem terribly quiet here this afternoon."

"It must have been welcome after the past wild days," he said.

"Not with what was in my mind."

The hard part was coming. He got up and started pacing the porch. "Come into the kitchen," he finally suggested. "Let's sit at the table and talk face-to-face."

"And then we'll have supper," she decided and went ahead to light a lamp.

He took his frock coat, hat, and tie and laid them on the horsehair sofa. She went back to the porch for the whiskey and glasses and poured a little in each. He built a cigarette and lighted it. She brought a saucer for an ash tray. He sipped his whiskey. She poured a little water in her glass. He went to the sofa and took the bank draft from his coat.

"This is yours," he said and laid it in front of her. "I'll endorse it and you can deposit it Monday. It would have been yours in any event. I had a purpose in mind when I had it made out in my name. It was all part of my plan to establish Franklyn Bye as a substantial citizen in Virginia City before I asked you to marry me."

"Did you ask me to marry you, Frank?" She hadn't looked at that check or heard anything else.

"I was going to." Once he'd told her the rest, he'd never be able to marry her. That was the test of himself, telling her and knowing what it meant. "I can't."

"Oh Frank, you're already married," she cried.

"No," he said sadly. "Far worse than that. You are a very wealthy woman. I can't ask you to marry me now."

"Wealthy?" She looked at the check for the first time. "But it's yours, Frank. Wherever did you get so much money?"

"You didn't hear what I said," he said miserably. He didn't want to go over it again. "It is your money. I only had it put in my name so I could start an account. So I could stay here without people ever questioning Franklyn Bye."

"You're talking nonsense," she said briskly. "Where would I get such a vast sum?"

He started to pace the floor in the kitchen. If it were only the seventeen thousand, eight hundred and fifty dollars, he could marry her and live with it. He could equal that amount in a few years with what he produced on the irrigated bench. It was the lode in the cave that stood between them. He had to tell her about it. It belonged to her.

It was her right to know. What was to be done with it was her decision to make.

He stood behind his chair facing her. "Eli had a bag of gold hidden in the cave. I found it. That's where this money has come from."

"Eli never told me anything about gold," she said. "It doesn't matter about him. You found it and told me."

"It's not just this," he said, indicating the check. "There's a cave within the cave. A cave with a lode of pure gold. You can go in there and dig out a thousand dollars or ten thousand dollars any time you want. You are enormously wealthy. You are worth millions of dollars. The quartz in the hill is shot with gold, like the Comstock. Do you understand what I'm saying? I can't ask you to marry me. There would always be doubt. All that gold would be between us. Did I marry you for your money?"

"Frank, darling," she said and got up and went to him. She hugged him and kissed him again and again. "What you've said is too fantastic to believe but I do accept it because you've told me so. It's because of the gold you can ask me to marry you. You told me about it. You didn't have to. It could have been yours alone and your secret all of your life. I'd never have known. You felt it stood between us and it tortured you and you still told me." She went to the table and picked up the check. "There is more than enough money here for all that we'll need. We can add onto this house or build a new one. We can irrigate the bench as you planned it and live well from what we raise. We don't have to touch the gold in the cave. I don't want to. It's cost three lives already. Can we seal it off, Frank?"

He was exhausted, emotionally drained, and happy and grateful. "I'd hoped you might say something like that. There's a granite slab in the tunnel to the gold. If I blast it with dynamite, there'd be no way to get at the gold. Come to think about it, we couldn't have a gold mine in there in any event. I want to use the cavern as a storeroom for vegetables."

Across the table from him in the lamplight, the imps came into her eyes and she laughed mischievously. "Are we through with the talking?"

"I haven't asked you to marry me," he said, beginning to smile.

"Oh yes you did!"

He chuckled. "I said I was going to ask you. Ever since then, you've been convincing me I could."

"Well, ask."

"No, I'm going to accept."

There was happiness in her eyes, and gaiety and mirth. "It's settled, then. I'll fry the steak." She paused. "Oh."

"What is it?"

"I left the steak in the cave so it wouldn't spoil."

"I'll get it. Where is it?"

"It's dark now."

"It's always dark in the cave," he said. "I'll take a lantern."

"Yes," she said. "And Frank?"

"Yes."

"Bring your fiddle. Will you play for me after supper?"

"I'll play gypsy music for you while you eat. A lullaby afterward. I'll play for you the rest of my life."

Frank was wearing his old clothes when he came back with the steak and the fiddle. After they'd eaten, they went out on the porch. It was beginning to cool a little and the westerly breeze was picking up. She sat in the rocking chair and he in a spool-backed straight chair he'd brought from the kitchen. He tucked the violin under his chin after he'd tuned it. His fingers danced on the fingerboard, and his bow flew over the strings. He did not tap his toe.

"Oh," she breathed softly minutes after he'd stopped. "That was lovely and gay and spirited. It didn't sound like the music you fiddled before. What was it?"

"Brahms. His Fifth Hungarian Dance." He tuned the violin once more and when he touched the strings this time, the melody was haunting and found a place in the heart. He was playing "Meditation" from Thaïs.

A breeze had started scampering through the streets of Virginia City when twilight crept through the town. At the jailhouse, the deputy stepped onto the stoop for a moment. Fargo looked up indifferently when Bart returned to the office. The marshal felt no interest in anything.

"It's cooled some, Cyrus," the deputy said. "Whyn't you get away for a hour or so? You been sitting in that chair all day and you look like you could do with fresh air. This being Saturday, we're going to have our hands full later."

"You get the new bars cemented in the pen window?" Fargo asked.

"Course I did, yesterday." Bart sounded exasperated. "You didn't hear what I said. You ought to get away for a spell afore business picks up. Take a little ride. Maybe it'll shake some of the misery out of your head."

"Maybe you're right," Fargo said. "I've been brooding a lot. I think I'll take a ride out of town."

He gave the mustang his head on the stage road. He rode north for almost an hour, well beyond the Diamond C. The wild gallop had invigorated him and restored his confidence. He was feeling more like his old self again when he wheeled the horse and started back to town at a lope.

25

His head was up and there was a faint smile on his lips as he approached the Widow Carrington's place. Bart had been right. He'd needed the ride and now was capable again of administering justice with a firm hand. Then he heard the strings again, at the same spot in the road he'd heard them before. Abruptly, he pulled the mustang to a halt and sat listening. The Fiddler was back. Fargo was motionless a moment, looking up the slope to the house where a small point of light showed. The wind was carrying the music from the widow's porch.

He listened intently and then he relaxed. A sad smile came to his lips. It wasn't the Fiddler, he realized. He still was obsessed. The Fiddler never had played anything like what he was hearing. He shook the mustang back into a lope, not entirely displeased with the beautiful music he was capable of making in his head.

And in the little house on the top of the slope where a lamp was turned low, Frank put the violin aside and took Boots in his arms.